Paging Help

"Oh, man! This is something else!" Joe exclaimed. He stepped inside and looked around. "It's like a hobby fantasy room!"

Frank was right behind him. "It looks like you got some new equipment, too," he said. "This is really—"

Just then one of the speakers in the room crackled and a voice said, "Calling KTRL492, calling KTRL492. Chet, it's Darren. If you're there, please sign on. We're in Hudson's Hope, British Columbia. In case you don't know, that's Canada. We're not who you thought we were, Chet. Get this message to Frank and Joe. We need their hel—"

Suddenly the radio went silent.

Frank and Joe looked at each other.

"What was that all about?" Chet said.

"Right now, I don't know," Joe said, "but I think we need to find out."

The Hardy Boys Mystery Stories

#109 The Prime-Time Crime
#110 The Secret of Sigma Seven
#139 The Search for the Snow Leopard
#140 Slam Dunk Sabotage
#141 The Desert Thieves
#143 The Giant Rat of Sumatra
#152 Danger in the Extreme
#153 Eye on Crime
#154 The Caribbean Cruise Caper
#156 A Will to Survive
#159 Daredevils
#160 A Game Called Chaos
#161 Training for Trouble
#162 The End of the Trail
#163 The Spy That Never Lies
#164 Skin & Bones
#165 Crime in the Cards
#166 Past and Present Danger
#167 Trouble Times Two
#168 The Castle Conundrum

#169 Ghost of a Chance
#170 Kickoff to Danger
#171 The Test Case
#172 Trouble in Warp Space
#173 Speed Times Five
#174 Hide-and-Sneak
#175 Trick-or-Trouble
#176 In Plane Sight
#177 The Case of the Psychic's Vision
#178 The Mystery of the Black Rhino
#179 Passport to Danger
#180 Typhoon Island
#181 Double Jeopardy
#182 The Secret of the Soldier's Gold
#183 Warehouse Rumble
#184 The Dangerous Transmission
#185 Wreck and Roll
#186 Hidden Mountain
The Hardy Boys Ghost Stories

Available from ALADDIN Paperbacks

THE HARDY BOYS®

#186

HIDDEN MOUNTAIN

FRANKLIN W. DIXON

Aladdin Paperbacks

First Aladdin Paperbacks edition August 2004
Copyright © 2004 by Simon & Schuster, Inc.

ALADDIN PAPERBACKS
An imprint of Simon & Schuster
Children's Publishing Division
1230 Avenue of the Americas
New York, NY 10020

The text of this book was set in New Caledonia.

Printed in the United States of America
2 4 6 8 10 9 7 5 3 1

Library of Congress Control Number 2003114271

ISBN 0-689-86737-9

Contents

1 The Strange Short Wave Message   1
2 We Have to Find Darren!   10
3 Storm Warnings   20
4 Danger in the Forest   31
5 The Empty Cabin   41
6 Intruders   47
7 Escape   57
8 Surrounded   71
9 The New Plan   83
10 Bear Attack   91
11 Saving the Wilkersons   103
12 Danger on the Trail   114
13 Falling Rocks   123
14 Hidden Mountain   136
15 Witness Protection   147

1 The Strange Short Wave Message

"Now, that's how I want to spend our next school vacation," Chet Morton announced to Frank and Joe Hardy as the three of them slowly made their way out of Theater Thirty in Bayport's newest movie complex. "Mountain climbing!"

They had just seen *Thin Air*, a film about the dangers of scaling the highest peaks of the Andes Mountains in South America.

"You and me both," Joe Hardy said. "You're living with danger twenty-four hours a day." He suddenly stretched his six-foot-one-inch frame above the throng heading toward the huge lobby and said, "Hey! I think that's Iola and Callie up there!"

Although neither one of the Hardy boys was in a serious relationship, from time to time Joe dated

Iola Morton, Chet's sister, and Frank dated Callie Shaw.

"Let's find out what they went to see," Frank said. An inch taller than Joe, he was able to act as a human periscope and lead the way. But it was Joe who was finally able to get Iola's attention with a wave. Iola, Callie, and a couple of other girls Joe recognized from Bayport High School maneuvered their way to the side of the corridor to wait for them.

"Which movie did you see?" Frank asked when he and his friends got to where the girls were standing.

"You'd call it a 'chick flick,'" Callie teased. "We girls would call it a serious look at male-female relationships."

"Uh-huh," Frank said. "I'm sure you would." He unconsciously finger-combed his dark brown hair and nodded to the two girls who were standing with Callie and Iola. "Janis and Stephanie, right?"

The girls blushed and nodded.

"So," Joe said, "what are you girls planning to do for the rest of the evening?"

"We're having a sleepover at my house," Callie said. She grinned. "We were planning to call up some boys later," she added. "Would you like to be on our list?"

Chet let out a groan.

"Mrs. Morton promised us snacks after the

movie," Joe said. "Our mouths will probably be too full to talk."

Iola ruffled Joe's blond hair. "Never get between a man and his stomach, right?"

"Right," Chet said.

"We need to run," Callie said. "My car's in the shop, so Dad's picking us up, and he doesn't like to sit and wait."

"See you!" Iola said.

"See you!" Frank and Joe said.

After the girls were gone, Frank noticed an exit off the corridor. "I think this'll be faster," he said.

The three of them headed down the almost deserted hallway toward a red exit sign. The door opened into parking lot J.

"We're in H," Joe said. "It should be just around the corner."

They quickly found the Hardys' van and lined up with the other departing vehicles to exit onto one of Bayport's major thoroughfares.

The traffic crawled for a couple of blocks until the theater traffic began to disperse. Frank was able to drive faster as they headed toward Chet's house in the older part of Bayport.

"I sure am hungry," Joe said. "I hope your mother made some of her famous spinach-artichoke dip."

"She did," Chet said, "and I saved a little of it for you."

"Thanks, Chet," Frank said.

"I can't get that movie out of my head. I could go see it again," Joe said. "I wish Darren Wilkerson could have been with us."

"Now *he* would have really liked it," Chet said. "Have you guys heard from him yet? I haven't."

"We haven't either," Frank said. "I thought we would have by now. He promised he'd let us know where they were moving."

"I keep thinking there's something strange about that," Joe interjected. "I mean, Darren called us up late one night and said that they were moving because of his father's business—and the next day they were gone."

"I never did know exactly what Mr. Wilkerson did for a living," Chet said. "He was always at home."

"Well, some people have home-based businesses," Frank said, "but they're not usually so secretive about them."

"If Darren ever *does* call, I'll tell him about the movie we just saw," Joe said. "I know he'll want to go see it."

"That's for sure," Chet said. "Turn here, Frank, because they're digging a sewer line on the next street over and you can't get through."

Frank turned the van at the next corner, drove two blocks, turned again, and made his way back to Chet's street.

"In fact, his parents would probably enjoy the movie too, since they seem to be interested in

4

mountain climbing," Joe said. "Remember how right before they left they started practicing on the cliffs above Barmet Bay?"

"Yeah," Chet said. "It was like all of a sudden they got the bug."

In his mind's eye, Joe could still see the Wilkersons as they scaled the rocky outcroppings that formed a semicircle around Barmet Bay. It had all started, he remembered, about two weeks before the Wilkersons moved from Bayport. At first they were very tentative in their climbs, but they gradually gained confidence and were soon going up and down the sheer cliffs as though they were old hands at it. Joe remembered being impressed and saying so to Darren. At the time Darren dismissed his compliments and changed the subject. Joe thought that he just didn't like people bragging about what he could accomplish, but now that he thought about it, it was more like Darren didn't want anybody to know he and his family were developing that skill.

Finally they reached the Mortons' house, and Frank pulled the van into the driveway behind Chet's car.

Frank liked the Mortons' part of town. The houses were older, but they had their own personalities, unlike some of the newer additions in Bayport, which seemed like they were made with the same cookie cutter.

Mrs. Morton greeted them at the front door. "Thank goodness, you're here!" she said. "I didn't think I'd be able to keep Mr. Morton away from the snacks much longer!"

A hearty laugh from the kitchen told the Hardy boys and Chet that that was a joke.

Chet looked at Frank and Joe and rolled his eyes. "Mom's not really joking," he said. "Dad loves junk food."

Mrs. Morton gave him a disapproving look. "*Junk* food! I'll have you know, Chet Morton, that your mother does not serve *junk* food in this house."

"Sorry, Mom," Chet said. "I just meant we weren't having roast beef, mashed potatoes, and green beans."

"Well, all right," Mrs. Morton said. "Now come along and fill up your plates so Chet can show you his surprise."

"Mom!" Chet said.

"Oops," Mrs. Morton said. "I guess I gave it away."

Frank and Joe looked at each other.

"What's this?" Frank said.

"Let's get our food first, and then I'll show you," Chet said. He looked at his mother. "There are no surprises in this house. You should see how it is around birthdays and holidays. We never had to worry about shaking presents to find out what was in the box, because Mom always did it for us!"

"I was just keeping up a family tradition," Mrs.

Morton said with a grin. She opened the door to the kitchen to reveal a table filled high with snacks. "How does this look?"

"Good grief, Mom!" Chet cried. "You're not feeding an army."

"Well, you *have* been known to eat like an army, Chet," Mr. Morton said, "so your mother didn't want you to be disappointed."

"It really looks great, Mrs. Morton," Frank said. "Thanks for going to all this trouble."

"I second what Frank said," Joe told her. "I'm starved."

Mrs. Morton handed them all paper plates. "I expect this to be eaten tonight," she said. "You're all still growing boys. You need your nourishment."

"That's what I'm all about," Chet said.

With Mrs. Morton encouraging them, the Hardy boys and Chet heaped their paper plates full of chips and dip, egg rolls, tacos, and small pizzas.

"Don't forget to take some of these crudités, too," Mrs. Morton said.

"These *what*?" Chet said.

"That's French for cut-up vegetables that you can use for dips," Mrs. Morton said. "It'll make me feel better if you have some vegetables with all of this other *junk* food."

The Hardy boys laughed.

Frank added some carrots and cucumber slices to his plate, while Joe took some green bell peppers and cauliflower. Chet grudgingly picked up a celery stick and put it in his mouth.

"Now the surprise," Chet said, leading the Hardy boys out the back door.

"We're going to eat on the patio?" Joe asked.

"Much better," Chet said. "But you'll never guess, so you might as well stop trying."

With Chet in the lead, the three of them crossed the backyard until they reached a newly built room attached to the back of the Morton's two-car garage.

"How'd this get here?" Joe asked.

"Dad did it in his spare time," Chet said.

"I knew it, Chet," Frank said. "They've finally moved you out of the house."

Chet snorted. "Yeah, right," he said. He set his plate on a concrete step and took a key out of his pocket. He unlocked the door, stuck his hand through, and turned on a light switch. A room full of shortwave equipment was illuminated.

"Oh, man! This is something else!" Joe exclaimed. He stepped inside and looked around. "It's like a hobby fantasy room!"

"It is! I was talking to a friend in South Africa before we went to the movies, and I didn't have time to shut everything down," Chet said, "but this way, it's all ready for me to show you how it works."

Frank was right behind him. "It looks like you got some new equipment, too," he said. "This is really—"

Just then one of the speakers in the room crackled and a voice said, "Calling KTRL492, calling KTRL492. Chet, it's Darren. If you're there, please sign on. We're in Hudson's Hope, British Columbia. In case you don't know, that's Canada. We're not who you thought we were, Chet. Get this message to Frank and Joe. We need their hel—"

Suddenly the radio went silent.

Frank and Joe looked at each other.

"What was that all about?" Chet said.

"Right now, I don't know," Joe said, "but I think we need to find out."

2 We Have to Find Darren!

"Let me see if I can raise anyone in Hudson's Hope," Chet said. He sat down in a chair in front of his huge shortwave radio, grabbed the microphone, and said, "This is KTRL492 in Bayport. I need to talk to anybody in the vicinity of Hudson's Hope, British Columbia. Anybody."

Just watching Chet in action impressed Joe. He liked what you could do with a shortwave radio. Over the years, he and Frank had solved a couple of mysteries that involved shortwave radios, but it was almost always the bad guys who used them. Now, Joe thought, maybe a shortwave radio could help *them* solve a mystery.

As Chet continued to try to reach someone in Hudson's Hope, Joe remembered that from time to time he had even thought about getting some equipment himself. When he mentioned it to Chet once, Chet got excited and promised to help him pass the test to get his shortwave license. But too many other things, like solving mysteries, intervened.

Chet looked up at them. "I can't get anybody to answer," he said. He rolled his chair over to a small computer, booted it up, and checked the weather for British Columbia.

"This might be the reason we lost the transmission," Chet said. He pointed to the screen. "They're having bad storms all over the northern part of the area."

"Or somebody could have just pulled the plug," Frank added. "Somebody who didn't want Darren broadcasting that information."

The three of them looked at one another.

"Remember when we were talking about them earlier, when we thought maybe there was something odd about their leaving Bayport so fast like that?" Joe said. "Well, we may have hit the nail on the head!" He thought for a minute. "Aren't there a lot of mountains in British Columbia?"

"*Mountain climbing!*" Frank said. "We need to talk to Dad about this." He looked at Chet. "I hate to cut this visit short, buddy, but I think this needs our immediate attention."

✵ ✵ ✵ ✵

Frank backed the van out of the Mortons' driveway and headed across Bayport to the Hardys' house. As soon as they got there, they went straight to their father's study.

"Come in, come in," Fenton Hardy told them. "I can tell by the look on your faces that you've just found a mystery that needs solving."

It was clear to the boys that their father had been working.

Fenton Hardy was one of the world's best known detectives. His expertise was sought by police departments not only in the United States but in almost every other country in the world.

"You remember Darren Wilkerson, Dad?" Frank said. "He and his family lived here for several months, then suddenly moved away a few weeks ago."

"We had him over at the house a few times," Joe added.

"Of course I remember him," Mr. Hardy said. "He was a nice young man. Is he having some kind of a problem?"

"We're not sure," Frank said. He told Mr. Hardy about the shortwave radio message Chet had received. "The weather could have caused problems with the transmission . . . or somebody could have stopped him."

"I know he was about to ask us to help him, Dad," Joe said. "He sounded scared. Didn't he, Frank?"

Frank nodded. "He really did, Dad," he said.

Fenton Hardy took a world atlas off a bookshelf, opened it up to a map of British Columbia, and located Hudson's Hope. "It's near Dawson Creek," he said. "I say we notify the authorities there and have them investigate."

"I don't think that's a good idea, Dad," Joe said. "I'm sure the reason that Darren called us is because he trusts us. I have a feeling that the police might scare them."

"Well, I've got a good friend who's a private detective in Dawson Creek—Rupert Kitimat," Mr. Hardy said. "I could telephone him and ask him to look into the matter, if you'd like."

Frank and Joe looked at each other.

"Well, we sort of had something else in mind, Dad," Joe said. "We have a school vacation coming up, and we thought that we'd fly up to Hudson's Hope and look into it ourselves."

"After all, we have a pretty good record of solving mysteries," Frank added, "and this one is personal, because of our friendship with Darren."

Fenton Hardy pondered the request for a moment. Finally he asked, "What's involved here?"

"I won't lie, Dad," Joe said. "There could be some mountain climbing."

"Mountain climbing?" Fenton Hardy said. He frowned at the Hardy boys. "How do you know?"

Joe described how just a few weeks before the Wilkersons left Bayport they had suddenly taken an interest in mountain climbing. "They were up and down those cliffs around Barmet Bay almost every day."

"Now we think it was practice," Frank added. "Something must have happened to them to make them believe they needed to know how to climb a mountain."

"There are a lot of mountains in British Columbia," Joe added.

"I don't know, boys," Mr. Hardy said. "I'm not completely sold on this adventure."

"It's not just an adventure, Dad," Joe said. "Frank and I really do believe that Darren and his family are in trouble."

"And climbing a mountain might not even be necessary," Frank said, "but if it is, we would need to be prepared to do it—if it meant solving this mystery."

Fenton Hardy looked at his watch. "British Columbia is on Pacific Time, three hours behind us, so it's not too late to call Rupert in Dawson Creek. I need to finish what I was doing when you guys got here, so I'll do that and then call Rupert."

"I've got an English paper that's due tomorrow," Joe said. "I can work on that."

"And I have a few calculus problems left to do," Frank added.

"Okay. You guys take care of your homework," Mr. Hardy said, "and I'll let you know what Rupert says."

As Frank and Joe started down the hall toward their room, their aunt Gertrude was coming from the other direction. She was wearing her robe and had a strained look on her face.

"What's wrong, Aunt Gertrude?" Joe asked.

"Oh, I just had the most disturbing telephone call from a old friend of mine in Wisconsin," Aunt Gertrude said. "Her house burned down and the insurance won't pay for it."

"Why not?" Frank asked.

"Well, her husband hadn't paid the premiums for six months, and she didn't know about it," Aunt Gertrude said. "She's mentioned in several letters that he's been getting forgetful about things, but nothing like this has ever happened before." She shook her head sadly. "Now my friend thinks her husband may be in the initial stages of Alzheimer's."

"Oh, that's too bad," Joe said. "It's a terrible disease."

Aunt Gertrude nodded and started on down the hall toward the kitchen. "I need a cup of tea. That usually soothes me," she said. "Good night, boys."

"Good night, Aunt Gertrude," Frank and Joe said.

Once they were in their room, Frank plopped down on his bed with his calculus book and finished doing all of the problems in the exercise he had started right after school.

Joe booted up the computer, put a disk into the drive, opened up the file with his English paper, and, using his notes, started typing the last few pages.

Several minutes later Mr. Hardy knocked on their door and came inside. He sat down on the bed next to Frank.

Joe quickly saved the changes to the file, clicked the print button, and turned around. "I hope you've got good news," he said.

"Well, I think I do," Mr. Hardy said. "Rupert was at home when I called him. I told him what I knew of the situation—what you boys told me, that is— and he suggested that he make a couple of discrete telephone calls to friends of his in Hudson's Hope. He just called me back."

"What did he find out, Dad?" Frank asked.

"Hudson's Hope is a small town, but there are a lot of tourists there because of Lake Williston—so it's hard to keep track of people who are just in town for a few days," Mr. Hardy said, "but Rupert said that a family fitting the description of the Wilkersons has been in town for several weeks."

"Bingo," Joe said.

"Rupert was also able to get an address," Mr. Hardy added.

Frank sat up. "That's even better, Dad!" he said.

"That's what I thought, too," Mr. Hardy said.

"So are you saying that we can go to British Columbia to find out for ourselves what the Wilkersons' trouble is?" Joe asked.

"I discussed that with Rupert," Mr. Hardy said. "He's agreed to be your safety backup."

"Safety backup?" Frank said. "What does that mean?"

"It means that since your parents won't be close by, there'll be somebody you can call on in case of serious trouble," Mr. Hardy said.

"Oh, come on, Dad," Joe protested. "Frank and I have been in tight situations before, and we've always managed to get out of them."

"I know, I know, but somehow I have a feeling this is different," Mr. Hardy said. "In any case, those are the rules, and if you want to take on this particular mystery, you have to abide by them."

"I can live with them," Frank said.

Joe nodded. "I guess I can, too."

"Well then, I'd say that tomorrow you two should go down to Bayport Extreme Sports Gear and get some mountain climbing equipment," Mr. Hardy said. He handed Frank a list. "Here's what Rupert suggested. If you can't find it all here in Bayport, then you can pick up anything else you need once you get to Canada."

Joe gave Frank a big grin. "We're going to British Columbia," he said. "We're going to live that movie!"

"Movie?" Mr. Hardy said.

"We went with Chet tonight to see *Thin Air*," Frank said. "It was about mountain climbing in South America."

"And Dad, the funny thing is that we had been talking about how much we thought Darren would enjoy it—because of his family's interest in mountain climbing—when we heard his message on Chet's shortwave radio," Joe added. "Weird."

The next day, Friday, was the last day before the school break, so it was hard for anyone to keep his or her mind on anything academic. In fact most of the teachers just let everyone sit around and talk.

Joe was glad. All he could think of was what he and his brother would do once they got to British Columbia. In fact he could hardly wait for the last bell so he and Frank could go to Bayport Extreme Sports Gear to buy their mountain climbing equipment.

They had asked Chet to go with them, but he said his parents had told him to come straight home so he could finish packing for their trip to Santa Fe, New Mexico.

"I can't believe that you guys will be mountain climbing and I'll be going from one art gallery to another," Chet said.

"Really?" Joe said. "Why?"

"Yeah, Chet," Frank said. "Since when have you been interested in art?"

"I'm *not*," Chet said. "That's the thing! I'll just be carrying the paintings to our van."

"I don't understand," Joe said.

"My mother has decided that she's going to redecorate our house in 'New Mexico' style," Chet said. He shook his head. "We're going to have bleached cattle skulls on every wall, leather sofas that look like horse saddles, and . . . well, you get the picture."

"We'll be thinking about you," Frank said.

Chet rolled his eyes. "Yeah, I'm sure you will," he said. "Well, be careful. I'm looking forward to living your vacation vicariously when you get back—so don't have any serious accidents!"

The Hardy boys parted company with Chet in the school parking lot and headed toward downtown Bayport.

Just as they reached Bayport Extreme Sports Gear, another van pulled away from a parking space in front and Frank expertly parallel parked the van.

"Do you have the list?" Frank asked, pulling some coins out of his pocket to feed the parking meter.

Joe patted his breast pocket. "Right here," he said.

Bayport Extreme Sports Gear carried equipment for almost every sport a person could name, and it was one of the larger businesses in Bayport. The show windows on the street held dioramas of each sports activity. Frank and Joe found the one that had the diorama for mountain climbing. It showed two climbers making their way up the sheer cliff of a snow-covered mountain.

"In just a few days, that'll be us, Joe," Frank said.

"I know. And I can hardly wait," Joe said.

3 Storm Warnings

"JFK is this way," Joe said, pointing to the green traffic sign above the freeway.

Frank exited at the next right, made a sharp left, went back under the freeway, then made a sharp right. He followed that with a zigzag and another sharp right. "I'm glad traffic isn't heavy at this hour," he said. "This construction zone is confusing."

"With me as your navigator, you'll never have any problems," Joe said. He looked over and grinned at his brother. "We didn't get lost, did we?"

"Well, I'll have to hand it to you, Joe," Frank said. "The directions have been perfect so far."

"Plan for it to continue," Joe told him. He leaned forward and squinted. "I think that's the turnoff for long-term parking up ahead," he said.

"Yeah, I think I recognize the building—but we've never come in from this direction before," Frank said.

In another half block, there was a temporary sign pointing them to the long-term parking entrance. Frank turned onto the road, only to be faced with a line of cars.

"A security checkpoint," Joe said, looking at his watch. "Well, if this doesn't take too long, we'll be all right," he said, "but if there's somebody with anything suspicious, we're in trouble."

Fortunately everything went smoothly and Frank found a space on the fourth level of the parking garage.

Joe pointed to a sign on the far side of the building. "International terminal," he read.

The Hardy boys got their luggage from the back of the van and headed toward the terminal. After maneuvering through several construction detours they finally arrived and got in the check-in line for their flight to Edmonton, Alberta.

Just as they reached the counter, the agent said, "Frank and Joe Hardy?"

Joe looked at the young woman for a couple of seconds, then said, "Annie Wilson?"

The woman nodded and grinned. "I haven't seen you two boys since you were in junior high school!"

"You moved to New Jersey, that's why," Joe said to their former baby-sitter. He gave her a big smile.

Under her breath, Annie said, "I don't think the people behind you are too interested in our having a reunion here, so I'll just say it was great to see you, and I wish I had time to catch up on all you've been doing since I saw you last."

"We're still solving mysteries," Frank whispered.

"And we're on our way to Canada to solve another one," Joe added.

"I should have known," Annie said, smiling.

She quickly punched in the information from the e-mail confirmation that Frank handed her, looked at their IDs, which they gave her without being asked, and then handed them their two boarding passes.

"You're boarding at Gate F 10 in thirty minutes, but take your checked luggage to security first," Annie said. "It was so good to see you two," she added in a whisper. "You look great!"

"Same here, Annie," Frank whispered back.

"Next in line," Annie said.

The Hardy boys waved good-bye, then, with boarding passes firmly in hand, they got in a second line to have their checked luggage screened. The process went smoothly until the passenger right in front of them was taken away by the airport police.

"I wonder what that was all about," Frank said.

Joe shrugged.

Frank was hoping that none of their mountain climbing equipment, such as the ice axes and tools and the crampons, would raise any eyebrows—they certainly *looked* like they could be dangerous weapons. But they were told they had to check it.

As they headed for concourse F, Frank said, "My stomach's growling. Do you want to get something to eat?"

Joe looked at his watch. "Our flight to Edmonton will be boarding soon," he said, "but maybe we can find something quick on the way to the gate."

They found concourse F, had their carry-on bags screened, and then headed for gate 10.

"I knew we should have gotten something before we went through security," Frank said. "Look at the crowds at these snackbars. It'd take forever to get something to eat."

"Hey, wait, Frank," Joe said. He was looking at their boarding passes. "This is a meal flight—we're in luck."

Just as they reached gate 10, the agent began calling row numbers.

The Hardy boys got in line, and within just a few minutes they'd boarded the plane. And, as luck would have it, their third seat was unoccupied, so they were able to stretch out even more.

After the usual preparations, the airplane left the terminal, got in line for takeoff, and was soon racing down the long runway.

Everything about the takeoff was smooth—and once the plane was in the air, the Hardy boys couldn't have asked for more attentive service.

"This food is great!" Joe told one of the flight attendants whose nametag said she was Bonnie.

"Would you like seconds?" Bonnie asked him. "The flight's not full, so we have some trays left over."

"Well, Bonnie, my brother and I are kind of hungry," Joe told her with a grin, "so we'd love some more of whatever there is."

"My pleasure—hang on a minute," Bonnie said.

The seconds turned out to be steak from first class. Bonnie had brought another attendant with her, June, to help serve and for just a few minutes, the boys felt like royalty.

"Is Edmonton your final destination?" June asked.

"No, we're going on to Dawson Creek," Frank told her.

"Oh, that sounds like an adventure!" Bonnie said. "We're on a turnaround."

"What's that?" Joe asked.

"This flight just turns around in Edmonton and goes back to New York," June said. "We don't have a layover."

Just then a couple of bells rang, summoning Bonnie and June to other passengers.

"Call us if you need anything," Bonnie said. "We'll be back to get your trays in a while."

Joe looked over at Frank. "I think somebody's jealous that Bonnie and June were spending so much time with us," he said with a grin. "They probably rang them to complain."

"It's too late," Frank said. "I've already started eating my steak. They can't take it away!"

Joe took a bite of his steak. "Me too," he said.

Just as the brothers were finishing their second meal, the airplane entered some turbulence. The bumps lasted until they were almost to Edmonton, so Frank and Joe weren't able to continue their conversation with Bonnie and June, who, along with the rest of the crew, were kept busy attending to sick passengers. A male attendant finally retrieved their trays right before the plane touched down on the runway.

"Sorry we didn't get to talk to you some more," Bonnie told the Hardy boys as they exited the plane. "Maybe we'll see you on a future flight back to New York."

"I hope so," Joe said. He leaned over and whispered, "Save us some more of that steak."

"Okay," Bonnie whispered back. "Have a great time in British Columbia, and be careful!"

The Hardy boys hurried up the gangway and quickly found a monitor that told them where their Mountain Airways flight to Dawson Creek would be boarding.

"C 22," Joe said.

Frank looked around. "Well, we're in luck. We arrived at C 13, so we don't have too far to walk."

"We don't have a whole lot of time, though," Joe said. "I don't want to miss this flight. There's no telling what's happened to Darren and his family since we heard him on Chet's shortwave radio."

Weaving in and out of passengers walking in both directions, Frank and Joe finally arrived at C 22—just as the flight was boarding.

"It's a regional jet," Frank said. "We may not have as much room as on the flight from New York."

"It's just an hour, so I can stand it if we don't," Joe said.

They handed their boarding passes to the agent and hurried down the gangway.

"There are a couple of seats together at the back," an attendant at the door told them. "We're pretty crowded today. An earlier flight was canceled."

The brothers headed down the aisle and took the two seats on the left-hand side.

As the regional jet began pulling away from the gate, Joe tried to remember the map of western Canada that he had studied carefully as soon as they'd made the decision to go to Dawson Creek.

Since the weather couldn't have been better, Joe just assumed that the pilot would fly a direct route to Dawson Creek, which meant they'd head almost due northeast of Edmonton, flying over the vast forests of western Alberta. They were still just west of the massive Canadian Rockies, but Joe was sure that since he and Frank were sitting on the left-hand side of the plane that he'd be able to see some of the peaks in the distance.

Edmonton International Airport was south of the city, so once they were in the air, Frank and Joe could see the western suburbs of Alberta's capital. Soon they left the populated area, and then all Joe could see was a carpet of green.

The regional jet was noisier than the Air Canada plane they had taken from New York, so it made conversation difficult—the boys decided that it might be a good idea to get a little sleep before they got to Dawson Creek. Both of them liked to have white noise around them, so they kept a fan going in their bedroom back in Bayport all the time.

The next thing they knew, the flight attendant awakened the boys so they could put their seats in an upright position in preparation for the landing.

The Dawson Creek airport was small, so Frank and Joe didn't have to walk far to find Rupert Kiti-mat. Their father had described him perfectly—Frank and Joe recognized him instantly. He looked like a professional wrestler.

"We'll get your bags and put them on the pon-toon plane," Detective Kitimat said. "It's ready to leave when we are."

Frank and Joe looked at each other.

"That's great," Joe said. "I'm glad we're going right away."

"We've been worried that Darren and his family

might bolt again and we'd never find them," Frank added.

Detective Kitimat shook his head. "I called my contact just before I headed out to the airport," he said. "The Wilkersons are still in Hudson's Hope, but when my friend spotted the father in the supermarket earlier this morning, he seemed a little wary."

"Wary?" Frank said.

Detective Kitimat nodded. "When he got out of his car, he looked around like he was trying to see if anybody had followed him—and then he ran into the market," he said. "He more or less repeated that behavior on the way out."

"So you think that they may be ready to flee again?" Joe said.

Detective Kitimat shrugged. "It's hard to tell," he said. "Neither I nor my contact in Hudson's Hope is privy to what they might have done, if they have done anything—but I do know that there's no warrant out for their arrest."

Just then, the conveyor belt that had the luggage for the Hardy boys' flight started. It wasn't long before Frank and Joe's bags appeared. The Hardy boys reached out to grab them, but Detective Kitimat picked them both up as though they were empty.

"Save your strength. You've got a rugged trip ahead of you," Detective Kitimat said. "Anyway, we'll have to walk to the hangar with the pontoon plane, because I took a taxi out to the airport." He shook his head. "My car's in the shop with carburetor problems."

Frank was a little put off by the detective's offer to take the bags. He obviously didn't realize that Frank and Joe stayed in top physical shape by playing several sports at Bayport High School. Frank knew that the detective didn't mean anything personal by it, though, so he didn't argue. As it turned out, it really was a long walk to the terminal where the pontoon plane was—so in the end, Frank appreciated not having to carry all that mountain climbing equipment.

The pilot was standing beside the plane when the Hardy boys and Detective Kitimat arrived.

"This is Harry Dell. He's the best bush pilot around these parts," Detective Kitimat said. "He can land on almost any kind of water."

"Well, Williston Lake should be pretty easy," Harry said, "although there's a pretty bad storm headed that way."

Detective Kitimat raised an eyebrow. "Really?" he said. He looked at the Hardy boys. "Are you still set on hiking into Hudson's Hope? We could drive in if you'd like."

Joe shook his head. "If we can still land on the lake, Frank and I think that's our best bet," he said. "We don't want to arouse anyone's suspicions—and we think we would if we arrived by car. If we walk in, we think we'd be less conspicuous. Nobody would suspect us—they'd just think we were hikers."

"We don't think the Wilkersons will bolt if they see us," Frank said, "but if there's someone watching the Wilkersons and they find out that we're trying to reach them, then they might . . . well, we don't know exactly, but we do know that the Wilkersons seem to be afraid of somebody, and we don't want whomever it is tipped off as to what we're planning to do."

Detective Kitimat looked at the pilot.

Harry nodded. "If we hurry, we can beat the storm," he said. He opened the luggage compartment and helped the Hardy boys stow their things. "The two seats in the back are kind of cramped, but we won't be in the air for very long."

Frank and Joe climbed into the back seats, buckled up, and waited for the pilot to start taxiing down the runway.

Williston Lake was northeast of Dawson Creek, Joe knew. When he looked out the window in that direction, he only saw very thick, dark clouds.

4 Danger in the Forest

Frank had never been in a scarier takeoff. As the small plane lifted from the runway, it swung back and forth in the air like a carnival ride—and Frank's stomach started to feel queasy.

When Frank looked over at Joe, he could tell that Joe was feeling the same sensation.

Just then Harry looked over his shoulder. "You boys okay?" he asked.

Frank nodded. "Never been better," he managed to say.

"Same here," Joe shouted.

But the higher they climbed, the more turbulent the air was—and Joe began beating himself up mentally for not taking Detective Kitimat up on his suggestion to drive into Hudson's Hope. It would be better to take a chance on having someone see them than to die in a plane crash in the wilds of northern British Columbia.

"Actually, this isn't too bad," Detective Kitimat shouted. "I've been in worse."

"Really?" Joe said.

Detective Kitimat nodded.

For the next thirty minutes, the plane seemed to be blown all over the sky. Since Harry didn't act alarmed, though, Frank and Joe decided they wouldn't worry either.

"This outflow may seem scary," Harry finally told the Hardy boys, "but that over there," he added, pointing to what Frank thought were some really ominous looking clouds, "now, *that's* scary."

Finally Detective Kitimat said, "That looks like Williston Lake down there."

Out Frank's window, there was nothing but the tops of trees—but Joe said, "I see it." *At least if we lost all of our power now,* he thought, *we might still be able to land safely on the water.*

Harry began a sharp dive, then pulled up some—and within minutes they were on the lake.

The spray of water on the boys' windows kept them from seeing anything until the plane slowed. They were heading toward a small pier.

"I don't mean to cut and run like this, guys," Harry said, "but when we stop, you need to get out and unload your gear as fast as possible. I can just make it back into the air before the storm hits."

When the pontoon plane nudged the edge of the pier, Detective Kitimat quickly opened his door and jumped out. Frank and Joe followed. Together they unloaded their gear and shut all of the compartment doors.

When the boys were finished, Detective Kitimat gave Harry the okay sign. Harry revved the engines and roared away from the dock, forcing Frank and Joe to jump back to avoid getting sprayed with lake water.

A bolt of lightning struck something on the other side of the lake. Within moments, a loud crack of thunder almost split their eardrums.

"We can't stay here, boys," Detective Kitimat said. "We need to start for Hudson's Hope. The woods might give us a little protection when that storm hits."

"Will we be able to make it before dark?" Joe asked.

Detective Kitimat nodded. "This far north and west it's light until around 11 P.M., so we're okay as far as time's concerned," he said. "It's just dark because of the storm clouds. Fortunately these thunderstorms are fast movers— so if we can hang on for a couple of hours, we'll be just fine."

Frank and Joe followed Detective Kitimat's lead and removed their yellow rain panchos and hoods from their packs.

"We brought along maps and a compass," Frank said.

"Well, we shouldn't need them," Detective Kitimat said. "I've fished this lake and hunted these woods for years, so I pretty much know the entire area between here and Hudson's Hope."

"That sounds good to us," Joe said. He and Frank hefted their gear onto their backs and began following Detective Kitimat up the pier.

"These trees are thick," Frank said. "It looks like there's a lot of underbrush here, too."

Detective Kitimat nodded. "We've had a lot of rain these last few years," he said, "but with just one short drought this whole place would turn to firewood."

They left the wooden pier and immediately stepped onto a carpet of rocks covered by green algae. Ahead of them loomed a forest of spruce and fir.

Within moments they were surrounded by a swirling mist and it was impossible to see very far in front of them.

Frank turned to look at where they had come from. The lake had disappeared from view. He had the oddest feeling, too, as if he had entered a strange new country—a land that was only found in the tales of King Arthur and the Knights of the Round Table. It was a very odd sensation.

Suddenly a cloud of mosquitoes surrounded Joe's

head, and he frantically started swatting them away. They left, only to be replaced by some tenacious deer flies.

"Everything okay?" Detective Kitimat called.

Joe opened his mouth to answer but at that moment rain started falling in thin sheets between the narrow spaces where the trees didn't block out the sky.

Detective Kitimat led them to one of the larger trees, which allowed very little of the rain to penetrate.

"We've been down in a valley, but from here on into Hudson's Hope, it's a pretty steep climb," Detective Kitimat said. "It's challenging during good weather, but in a storm like this it could be downright dangerous." He stopped and looked at the Hardy boys. "We could make camp here and ride it out if you want. It should be all right."

Frank and Joe shook their heads at the same time.

"We're used to danger," Joe said. "I say we keep going. I really don't want to take a chance on the Wilkersons leaving Hudson's Hope while we're camping."

"Me either," Frank said.

"Then that's what we'll do," Detective Kitimat said. He gave them a big grin. "You're your father's sons, all right. That's what Fenton would have done too."

35

"We know," Frank and Joe said in unison.

Almost immediately the ground rose and the terrain became incredibly slippery. The three of them were soon almost crawling to keep from sliding backward. Fortunately there were plenty of roots to hold on to. Frank and Joe put their mountain climbing skills to use, thinking of the loose roots as footholds.

Suddenly Detective Kitimat stood up and put his hand to his ear, then turned and hunched down next to Frank and Joe. "Don't move," he whispered.

At that moment, a huge brown bear appeared in front of them. Frank couldn't believe its size. Two bear cubs came out from behind the mother and stood on either side of her.

Joe was glad for the rain—it meant their scents wouldn't be in the air and if they just stayed where they were, the mother might ignore them.

Unfortunately she reared up on her hind legs and roared. When the bear finally fell to the ground, Frank was sure he felt the earth shake.

"Start backing up slowly," Detective Kitimat whispered, "but don't take your eyes off of her."

Joe had just lifted his left foot when the two cubs suddenly broke away from their mother and went crashing through the woods.

The mother seemed just as puzzled by what had happened as the three of them were, and disappointed that now she'd have to chase after her offspring instead of enjoying a meal of the three intruders in front of her.

The bear gave one more roar and started after her cubs.

"This way!" Detective Kitimat whispered. "We need to get as far away from her as we can." With Detective Kitimat in the lead, they took off down the trail.

Joe wasn't sure if the rain had slacked off some or if having survived almost being attacked by a bear made walking through a forest in a downpour seem tame.

"What were the cubs after?" Frank asked.

"A chipmunk, probably," Detective Kitimat said. "They're still curious at that age."

"I guess we can thank that chipmunk for saving our lives," Joe said. "I hope it's smart enough to dive for cover before the cubs do any damage."

For the next hour, everyone concentrated on the job at hand: making it through the forest as fast as possible. The Hardys were set on reaching Hudson's Hope in time to find out what was going on with the Wilkersons. From time to time there would be a sudden burst of rain, but it had mostly turned to annoying drips.

Joe was amazed at how easily Detective Kitimat maneuvered the rough terrain. He seemed to know exactly when to zig and when to zag.

Frank had just glanced down at his watch and

saw that they were almost two hours into the trip, which meant that they should be getting close to Hudson's Hope. Just then Detective Kitimat dropped to the ground. "Hide!" he said. "Someone's coming. We shouldn't be seen."

Frank and Joe dived for cover in the closest underbrush and buried themselves as deeply as they could. At the same time another heavy cell of the storm was passing over them, which meant that once again they were subjected to torrents of rain. This time, without the shelter of the thick branches from the junipers and firs, the rain found its way to them—but for the most part the panchos kept the rain from soaking into their clothes.

When Detective Kitimat finally gave them the all-clear signal, Frank and Joe climbed out from under the brush—a little scratched up, but none the worse for wear.

"Who was that?" Joe asked.

"A family of campers," Detective Kitimat said.

"You don't think they're lost, do you?" Frank said.

"Maybe we should have helped them," Joe added.

"The father had a compass and seemed to know what he was doing," Detective Kitimat said. "I think they're all right."

Once again they resumed their trek toward Hudson's Hope. They had only climbed a few feet when they started going downhill. The Hardy boys used the roots as steps to keep from sliding.

"How much farther?" Joe asked Detective Kitimat.

"Not much," Detective Kitimat said.

A couple of minutes later he stopped, pulled aside some branches, and said, "Hudson's Hope, British Columbia."

"It looks like a nice, peaceful place," Joe said, "not someplace where something awful is about to happen to our friend Darren Wilkerson."

"Well, I'm not quite sure there's any place on Earth that doesn't have its share of trouble," Detective Kitimat said.

"I think Joe just meant that it's a shame that someplace so beautiful could be the setting for something awful," Frank said.

"Well, I have to agree," Detective Kitimat said. He undid a strap across his waist and let his gear slide to the ground. "I think we need to make a few plans."

"I agree," Frank said.

"First of all, how are we going to communicate?" Detective Kitimat said.

Joe took a couple of powerful walkie-talkies out of his backpack. "With these," he said. "Dad lent them to us. They're the best." He handed Detective Kitimat one of the walkie-talkies.

"We thought you could more or less shadow us," Frank said. "We don't want the Wilkersons seeing anybody but us so they won't be spooked—but it'd be great if you were close enough to help out in case things got out of hand."

"Dad thought that was a good idea," Joe added.

"I agree," Detective Kitimat said.

Frank shrugged. "After that we're just going to have to play it by ear," he said. "We really believe that Darren wanted our help, so that's why we're here—but we don't know a thing about what's going on with his family."

"Well, we *do* know one thing, I guess," Joe said. "Darren said that they weren't who they said they were."

"That sounds ominous," Detective Kitimat said. "As I told you, there are no warrants out for them, so we didn't think we could do too much more investigating."

"We're glad you didn't," Joe said.

The Hardy boys took off the yellow rain panchos, shook them out, and repacked them.

Joe looked at Frank. "Ready?" he said.

"Ready," Frank said.

"Then I say we head into Hudson's Hope and see if we can solve this mystery," Joe said.

5 The Empty Cabin

It was exactly 6 P.M. when the Hardy boys made it to Hudson's Hope. One moment they were deep within a forest, and the next minute they were on a sidewalk.

"They probably have a lot of nonhuman visitors," Frank remarked. "There's nothing to keep out bears or deer or whatever else shows up."

"The residents must like it like that," Joe said. "I think it's kind of neat."

"Well, Detective Kitimat seemed to think that our plan made sense, that if we came into town this way, people would just think we were returning from a day of hiking," Frank said, pulling out a map. "We just need to make sure we don't do anything to give ourselves away."

"I guess we could act like we're really tired. That certainly wouldn't be hard to do," Joe said. He looked at his watch. "We have about five hours before it gets dark. That should be enough time to find out what we need to know."

As they continued down Wilderness Road, Frank said, "This map that Detective Kitimat drew for us shows that the street we need is called Pine. The Wilkersons' house is number 27."

"That street sign up ahead says Fir Trail," Joe said.

"Yeah, that's on here," Frank told him. "Pine is the next street."

"Maybe we shouldn't go straight to the Wilkersons' house," Joe said. "Let's just make a little detour through the area to find out if we're being watched."

"Good idea, Joe," Frank said.

The Hardys continued down Wilderness Road toward what they were sure was the center of Hudson's Hope. There were a few residents about, but no one paid any real attention to them.

When they reached the edge of the small downtown area, they looked in some of the store windows, like any other good tourist would do. After a short time they began doubling back toward their original destination.

Finally they came to the intersection of Wilderness Road and Pine Street.

"Let's just make a turn as though we've done this before," Frank said under his breath.

"Right," Joe said.

Although Pine Street was paved, it wasn't much wider than a hiking trail, and, from what the Hardys could see, it looked as though it led back into the forest. The houses, most of which were log cabins of varying sizes, were built to blend in with the surroundings.

After having walked the equivalent of three blocks, Frank and Joe finally found number 27.

"If the Wilkersons are looking out a window, I hope they can tell who we are," Joe said. "I'm starting to wonder what I look like after that hike in from Lake Williston."

"You still look like Joe," Frank said.

"And you still look like Frank," Joe said.

"Well, good!" Frank said.

When Frank and Joe got to the front of number 27, they took a dirt trail that led up to the front porch.

"I thought somebody would have greeted us by now," Joe whispered. "Are you sure I look like myself?"

"Positive," Frank whispered back. "Maybe they're not home."

"Maybe they've already left," Joe said.

Frank didn't like to think that might be the case. "I have a feeling that Detective Kitimat's friend here would have seen them heading out of town and reported it to him," he said. He suddenly thought of

43

something. "Unless they somehow knew he was watching them and figured out a way to avoid him."

"The door's open," Joe said as they started up the steps to the front porch.

"That might not mean anything," Frank said. "This could be the kind of town where people leave their houses unlocked."

Joe reached for the front door, opened it, and stepped inside. Frank was close behind.

"Darren!" Joe called out. "It's Joe and Frank Hardy."

They waited for the Wilkersons to appear, in case they had been hiding somewhere in the house. When no one showed after a few minutes, though, Joe looked around and said, "They may have gone out for supplies."

"Maybe," Frank said, but he was getting a bad feeling. "I say we look around to see what we can find."

"That's a good idea," Joe said. "If they come back, we can just tell them that we didn't think they'd mind if we came on inside."

Frank nodded.

For several minutes the Hardys surveyed the living room. It had the usual chairs and a sofa— nothing expensive. They were probably there when the Wilkersons moved in.

The only things that might have been considered out of place, Joe thought, were four suitcases in the corner of the room. "Let's check them out," he said. He went over and picked one up. "It's packed."

"They're either planning to leave soon, or they never unpacked from Bayport," Frank said.

Joe unzipped the suitcases. Three of them were full of clothes and other personal belongings, but one of them contained stacks of personal papers.

"Bank statements, passports, birth certificates, life insurance policies," Joe said. "You don't go off and leave things like this."

"They're getting ready to leave, Joe. I'm sure of it," Frank said. "They probably only went to the store to get some last minute items."

"Why are they running, Frank?" Joe said. "You don't think they're some kind of fugitives, do you?"

"Detective Kitimat said there were no outstanding warrants out on them, Joe," Frank said.

"That doesn't mean anything," Joe said. "What if they changed identities? The newspapers are always full of stories about people who committed crimes decades ago and are only now getting caught."

Frank sniffed. "What's that?"

"It smells like something's burning," Joe said.

The Hardys hurried to the kitchen. It was beginning to fill with smoke.

Frank ran over to the stove and turned off the burner. "A big pot of burned stew," he said. "And the burner was on low, so it's taken it a while to boil down."

"Something's not right here," Joe said. He was standing by the kitchen table. "I'd say the Wilkersons were interrupted in the middle of a meal by something . . . or *someone*."

Frank joined Joe at the table. "It looks like they just got up from the table and left," he said.

"I have an idea," Joe said. "Let's check out Darren's room."

There were only two bedrooms. Darren's was just off the kitchen. It was small, with barely enough room for a twin bed and a chest, but Frank and Joe recognized the posters on the wall.

Joe went immediately to the closet. "All of Darren's clothes are still here," he said.

On the top shelf, he found what he was looking for. "Darren's baseball card collection is worth a lot of money," he said. "He'd never go off and leave this unless . . ."

"Unless *what*? Frank said.

"Unless they were so scared by something that they literally just ran out of the house," Joe said.

Frank shook his head. "Now what do we do?" he said.

Joe sighed. "I don't . . ." Suddenly he looked around at the door to the bedroom. "Did you hear that? Somebody's coming."

"Quick!" Frank said. "Let's hide in Darren's closet!"

6 Intruders

The closet wasn't really big enough to hold two people the size of Joe and Frank, Joe knew, especially with the gear still strapped to their backs. But it was the only place they wouldn't be in full view if whoever was in the Wilkersons' house came into Darren's bedroom.

"Maybe it's just the Wilkersons," Joe whispered. "There could have been some kind of emergency. Maybe they just had to drop everything and leave—and now they've come back."

"I don't think so, Joe," Frank whispered back. "This place has a deserted look to it. The Wilkersons weren't planning on returning."

Just then, a man stuck his head through the door and said, "Nope! They're gone, that's for sure. We missed them. How are we going to explain this?"

Through Darren's shirts Frank could see the man's features. He looked like a prizefighter who had lost one too many bouts.

"Let's look around and see if we can find anything that might tell us where they went," a second man said.

Joe couldn't see the other man's face, but from the sound of his voice, Joe could tell that he was just a few feet behind the first man.

"Okay," the first man said.

"Well, that one guy looks like your worst nightmare—I'd hate to meet up with him in a dark alley," Frank whispered, "but they don't *sound* too threatening."

"That doesn't mean anything, Frank. They could still be planning to harm the Wilkersons," Joe said. "Darren and his family are scared of something, and it could be because of what they think these men might do to them."

"Joe!" Frank said in a loud whisper. "I just thought of something!"

"What?" Joe said.

"I can't believe I didn't connect the dots before," Frank said.

"What? What?" Joe said impatiently. "Tell me!"

"Remember on the trail, hiking into Hudson's Hope, when Detective Kitimat had us hide because some people were coming?" Frank said excitedly.

"Well, he said it was just a family of campers, probably trying to find their way back to their campsite."

"Oh, man! You don't think that was the Wilkersons, do you?" Joe asked. "I can't believe it."

"Well, the Wilkersons left this house in a real hurry," Frank said, "and I think they were running away again."

"But why through the forest, Frank?" Joe questioned him. "That doesn't make sense. Where would they be headed?"

"That's the mystery," Frank said. "And we've got to get out of this house so we can solve it."

"You're right," Joe said. "If that family was the Wilkersons, they've got a good head start on us. But those guys are still in the house—and they may stay here for a while."

"This room has a window, Joe," Frank said. "We'll just climb out that."

Joe maneuvered out from behind the clothes. The man who had looked into the room had left the door open, so Joe could still hear them talking. "It sounds to me like they're rummaging around, Frank—but I'm still going to close the door, just to make sure they won't be able to hear us when we leave," he whispered. "I doubt if that guy will remember whether he left it open or not."

"Just hope it doesn't squeak when you shut it," Frank said.

Joe tiptoed across Darren's room to the door.

Slowly he began to push the door towards its frame. He was able to get it almost closed, but not all the way.

Frank had been watching Joe carefully. When he could see that the door was almost shut, he maneuvered his way around Darren's clothes and tiptoed out of the closet to the window.

The window in the room was not one that a person had to push up, but one that you simply unlatched and pushed open like shutters.

Joe stuck his right leg through the opening, grasped the bottom of the frame, lifted his left leg over, and lowered himself to the ground.

Frank had just stuck his left leg out the window, when a voice shouted, "Hey! There's somebody in here!"

"Oh, man!" Frank said. He dived the rest of the way out the window and landed on his side, but he was up in seconds.

The man with the prizefighter face was now standing at the window. He was holding a gun. "They're getting away!" he shouted. "We've got to stop them!"

"We'll head straight into the woods, then try to circle back to where we came into town," Frank said. "I think I have a pretty good feel for how to do that."

"Okay," Joe said as he raced after Frank.

Both men left the house and took up the chase.

Joe could see that the second man also had a gun. He was surprised at how fast both of them could move, given their size, but he doubted they could keep up that pace very long. He and Frank were runners at Bayport High School. They were used to running long distances. Even with heavy backpacks on, Joe felt sure they could lose these two men. But just then a bullet whizzed over their heads, reminding Joe that no matter how fast they could run, they couldn't outrun a bullet.

Up ahead, Frank started zigzagging in and out of the trees. Joe did the same—but with his right hand, he pulled the walkie-talkie out of the side of his backpack. They needed to check in with Detective Kitimat. He silently berated himself for not doing it when they arrived at the Wilkersons' and found the house deserted. Of course, at the time they were still trying to decide exactly what had happened.

Joe pushed the talk button on the walkie-talkie. "This is Joe," he said. "Can you hear me?" He released the button and waited.

In just a couple of seconds there was a crackling noise, and a voice said, "Yes, but you sound out of breath. What's the problem?"

"We're running for our lives, that's what!" Joe said.

As quickly as he could, Joe told Detective Kitimat about finding the Wilkersons' house deserted and about hiding from the two men.

"They may be the reason the Wilkersons left in such a hurry," Joe said. "I can certainly understand that."

Joe had now pulled alongside Frank so his brother could be privy to the conversation with Detective Kitimat and to any decisions they had to make from here on out.

"Are you headed toward me?" Detective Kitimat said.

Frank shook his head.

Joe frowned. "We're not?" he mouthed to Frank.

Frank shook his head again. "Tell him that we think that family on the trail was probably the Wilkersons," he said. "Tell him we're going to backtrack, try to find them, and warn them about the two men."

Joe repeated the message to the detective.

"What do you want me to do?" Detective Kitimat said.

Joe handed the walkie-talkie to Frank.

"Just stay with us, but out of sight. If the Wilkersons really have been spooked, then they might not trust even Joe and me—especially if they see a stranger with us," Frank said. "You'll be our back-up, just as Dad planned it."

"I can do that," Detective Kitimat said.

Joe could hear the two men behind them, crashing through the forest—but they didn't seem to be getting any closer. It suddenly occurred to him that neither one of the men had fired another bullet. It also occurred to him that the first bullet might not have been meant to hit either one of them, but had just been fired as a warning. But a warning for what?

Just then Frank veered to the right, and Joe followed. Joe was pretty good at reading maps and finding shortcuts, but Frank had always been better at finding his way through wilderness, so Joe was happy to follow his lead.

"I think we're almost back to where we started," Frank said.

Sure enough, up ahead Joe saw a rock formation he thought he remembered from when they came into Hudson's Hope earlier.

"We're ready to start looking for the Wilkersons," Frank said. "This is the trail we came in on."

Detective Kitimat was nowhere in sight, but Frank had a feeling he was nearby.

"Let's pick up the pace," Frank said to Joe. "Pretend we're at the state track meet and we're trying to win all of the medals for Bayport High."

Joe grinned at him, put on a burst of speed, and said, "Pretend that *I'm* going to win all of the medals, you mean!"

"Yeah, *right*, little brother," Frank said. With his longer legs, he quickly caught up with Joe, but stayed even with him so they could still talk to each other.

Without the rain, it was easier to make more time.

Joe knew they had to be quick if they were going to find the Wilkersons in time. Their only hope was that the Wilkersons might have decided to wait out the weather under a canopy of trees for a while. Joe knew that he was only grasping at straws and that the Wilkersons could be miles away from them now—in which case the Hardys would never find them. Still, Joe told himself, there was no way they could give up.

All of a sudden, Frank stopped.

Joe was already a few feet ahead when he realized Frank had stopped. "What's wrong?" he asked his brother.

Frank had turned his left ear in the direction from which they had just come. "I'm listening," he whispered. After several seconds, he said, "I don't hear them, but that doesn't mean anything." He paused. "You don't think they're cutting through the woods, do you? They might know this place better than we think they do."

The idea of that sent chills down Joe's spine. He looked around, trying to see through the dense underbrush. "I don't know, but I don't think we should stay here wondering about it."

"You're right," Frank said. "Come on!"

The Hardy boys propelled themselves through the forest as fast as they could. Both Frank and Joe used their superior peripheral vision to look for any sudden ambush.

Up ahead of them they heard rushing water, and soon they were crossing a stream by way of a log bridge. Almost immediately they switched back up a narrow opening between two large rocks, only to find themselves once again confronted by dense forest.

"I don't remember coming this way, Frank," Joe said. "Do you?"

"Not really, Joe, but we're still on the trail," Frank replied. "It was raining, and we were concentrating so hard on following Detective Kitimat—admittedly, it never occurred to me then that we'd be coming back this way, so I wasn't really paying attention."

"Neither was I," Joe said.

"We shouldn't let that happen again," Frank said. "You never know what's going to happen when you're investigating a case. You have to be prepared for all possibilities."

Just as Joe started to nod his agreement, he felt himself being flung into the sky, swinging wildly, his body twisting in every imaginable direction. Pieces of woven twine were cutting into his skin.

"Joe!" Frank called from below. "Joe!"

Joe managed to move his head just enough to look down at the forest floor below and see Frank looking up at him.

"Are you okay?" Frank called.

"Am I *okay*?" Joe shouted down. "If hanging almost upside down in some hunter's net trap is okay, then I guess I am."

"I'll cut you down," Frank shouted.

"I have a simpler idea," Joe shouted.

Once again he managed to twist himself around inside the net and look up into the tree.

The net had been ingeniously set, but the hunter probably hadn't counted on trapping a human being. Joe stuck his fingers through the netting above and began pulling himself up toward the limb holding the trap. He was sure he could reach it, hoist himself up, and then cut himself free. As he climbed, however, he had a chilling thought: If Detective Kitimat was paralleling them, wouldn't he have shown himself and offered to help? They hadn't heard a word from him. Had they outrun him? Had they lost him? *As soon as I pull myself up on the branch,* Joe thought, *I'll use the walkie-talkie to try to contact him.*

Joe had only managed to climb a few feet when he stopped, stunned by what he could now see. From where he was hanging, he had almost a bird's-eye view of the part of the forest they had just come through. Not over a hundred yards behind them were the two men from the Wilkersons' house. That could be the reason Detective Kitimat hadn't come to their aid. He probably knew the two men were almost upon them, and had wanted to maintain his cover.

"Get ready, Frank," Joe called down to him. "We're going to have company."

7 Escape

The man who looked like a prizefighter was the first to arrive.

"FBI!" he shouted to Frank. "Get your hands up!"

Frank did as he was told—and exchanged a puzzled glance with Joe in the net trap above.

FBI? Joe thought.

The second man entered the clearing. His gun was pointed at Frank too, but he was looking at Joe swinging from the branch above him.

"What's going on here?" the second man asked.

"How do I know you're FBI agents?" Frank said, ignoring the second man's question. "You should have some identification to prove it."

Both men gave Frank a look that told him they really didn't want to prove anything to this teenager standing in front of them, but they both withdrew IDs from their pockets, flipped them open so Frank could see them, then put them back.

"Satisfied?" the prizefighter said. "I'm Agent Sims and this is my partner, Agent Martin."

"Yeah, I'm satisfied," Frank said. "My brother and I thought you might be . . ."

"We're not really interested in what your brother and you thought about us," Agent Martin interrupted. "We want to know what's going on with you two. What were you doing in the Wilkersons' cabin back there in Hudson's Hope?"

"What have you done with them?" Agent Sims said.

"Hey!" Joe called. "Remember me?"

"We need to get my brother down first," Frank said, "and then we can talk about this."

The two FBI agents looked back up at Joe, but neither one of them moved.

Frank took off his backpack, removed a hunting knife from a side pocket, and said, "Joe, if you can keep pulling yourself up to that limb, I'll be there to cut you free."

"Okay," Joe shouted down.

As Joe inched his way up to the branch that held the top of the net trap, Frank began climbing up the tree toward him. When Frank finally reached the branch, he edged his way out onto it until he was just above where Joe was hanging.

Frank grabbed the top of the net and helped pull Joe the rest of the way onto the branch.

"Those FBI guys aren't much help, are they?" Joe whispered.

"Not really," Frank whispered back as he began slicing through the net with his hunting knife, "but maybe they don't teach this stuff at Quantico."

"I guess not," Joe agreed.

Finally Joe was free of the net. He pulled himself up onto the branch and straddled it beside Frank.

"Are you okay? Any broken bones?" Frank asked. "That must have been a shock to your body."

"I'm okay, but I'll probably feel sore in the morning," Joe said. "I was mostly thinking about any poor animal who gets caught in one of these. They're no fun at all."

"Take off that backpack, Joe," Frank said. "I have an idea."

With Frank's help, Joe was able to remove the heavy backpack. "Wow!" he said. "What a relief!"

Frank cut the rest of the net from the branch and tied it around Joe's backpack, then he lowered it to the ground.

With that accomplished, the boys began edging their way back toward the trunk of the tree.

"You guys all right up there?" Agent Martin called. "Do you need any help?"

"We're fine," Frank shouted down to them. "Thanks, anyway."

When Frank and Joe were finally back down on the ground, Agent Martin said, "Now we need to have a little talk."

Joe shrugged. "Sure," he said. It kind of irritated him that neither agent seem all that interested in what he had just gone through.

"What do you want to know?" Frank asked.

"To start with," Agent Sims said, "what were you two doing at the Wilkersons' cabin?"

"They're friends of ours from Bayport," Joe said. "That's where we're from."

Frank glanced questioningly at his brother, but in a way that the two agents wouldn't notice. He could tell that Joe was about to give them an account that might not be entirely truthful—and he decided just to follow his brother's lead.

"We came up here because we've decided to leave home," Joe continued. "We wanted to hook up with them because they seem like free spirits who move around a lot."

"That kind of life appeals to us," Frank said. "We're tired of living such a dull existence in Bayport."

"That's interesting," Agent Martin said. "Did the Wilkersons tell you where they were coming after they left Bayport?"

"They mentioned British Columbia before they left," Joe said. "After they got here, Darren contacted us by shortwave radio and told us they were in Hudson's Hope."

The two agents were nodding as though they were trying to digest everything they were hearing.

Okay, Frank thought. *Joe's giving them just enough honest information so it's going to be hard for them not to believe us—but the rest of it he's just making up. I'm not quite sure what's going on here,* Frank decided, *but Joe must have latched onto something that isn't quite adding up.*

Meanwhile, Joe was having his own internal conversation. *Maybe I shouldn't have mentioned the shortwave radio,* Joe thought suddenly. *Now they'll probably ask me about that. I didn't see one in Darren's house. He must have met some kid in Hudson's Hope who let him use his. There are probably a lot of people in this part of the world who have shortwave radios.*

Agents Martin and Sims looked at each other and shrugged.

"Well, you guys seem honest," Agent Martin said, "so we're going to let you in on our little problem."

"Problem?" Frank said.

Agent Sims nodded. "It's very important that we find the Wilkersons because they're in danger—so if you know anything more about them than what you're telling us now, then you need to keep talking."

"What kind of danger?" Joe asked.

"Well, we can't tell you . . . ," Agent Sims started, but Agent Martin cut in. "Oh, I think we can trust these two guys to keep a secret. After all, they're friends of the Wilkersons, and they wouldn't want anything to happen to them." He stopped and looked at both Frank and Joe. "Would you?"

"Of course not," Frank said.

Agent Sims shrugged. "The Wilkersons have been in the government's Witness Protection Program," he said. "Mr. Wilkerson worked for a man who he didn't know was a gangster. When he found out, Mr. Wilkerson turned him in—but then he had to go into hiding because there were threats against him and his family."

Frank and Joe looked at each other.

"That makes sense," Joe said.

"What do you mean?" Agent Martin asked.

Frank was starting to be puzzled by these two agents. For one thing, they didn't seem as bright as most FBI agents. He guessed that maybe the kinds of assignments they were given—like running through the wilderness in places like British Columbia—didn't call for suits or degrees in accounting. Still . . .

"I just mean that it makes sense to go into hiding if people are trying to kill you, that's all," Joe said.

"The trouble is, the regular Witness Protection Program wasn't good enough," Agent Sims said. "The people who were after the Wilkersons kept finding them."

"Does that happen?" Frank asked.

"Of course it happens," Agent Martin said. "Some of these crooks are as smart as FBI guys."

"Oh, I don't know about that," Joe said. "I think most crooks are really dumb."

"Yeah?" Agent Sims said. "What do you know about it?"

"My brother and I have seen crooks before in Bayport," Joe continued. "None of them were very bright."

Frank was sure that Agent Sims was getting angry about this conversation, but he couldn't figure out why—unless he felt that Joe was questioning his expertise in the area of criminology.

"That's just my brother's opinion," Frank said. "We've just seen some crooks before—but we've never had anything to do with them." He looked at Joe. "Isn't that right?" he asked. "We don't really know anybody who's in law enforcement. We've just mostly seen a lot of this stuff on television."

"That's what I thought," Agent Sims said. He had a smug look on his face. "Well, I'm telling you that I know what I'm talking about, and some of these 'crooks,' as you call them, can outsmart any police officer or FBI agent in the country."

"Shut up!" Agent Martin said to him. "You talk too much."

Agent Sims' eyes flashed angrily.

Frank knew this whole thing was about to get out of hand, and he didn't like where it was all headed.

"Well, I believe you, sir," Frank said to Agent Sims. "You seem to know exactly what you're talking about." He looked around. "It's obvious to me that the FBI wants to help our friends the Wilkersons—and so do we. So what can we do to make sure they're okay?"

"Agent Sims and I were supposed to meet up with the Wilkersons in Hudson's Hope and take them to their new home," Agent Martin said. "It's a super secret place where nobody will ever find them. Only a few people in the government are even aware that it exists."

"Are you sure the Wilkersons didn't mention this to you?" Agent Sims asked.

"Positive," Frank said. "They didn't say a word about it."

"We didn't even know they were in the regular Witness Protection Program," Joe said. "Where exactly is this place, anyway?"

"Somewhere here in northern British Columbia," Agent Martin said.

"Do you have any idea where the Wilkersons are now?" Agent Sims asked. "From the looks of their house, they just got up and left."

Frank was thinking as fast as he could, trying to digest everything that was happening here. There was something about this whole episode that was making him very uncomfortable. He couldn't exactly put his finger on it, but it was there just the same. Two men who had identified themselves as FBI agents were looking for their friends the

Wilkersons. Frank actually believed what the men were saying, because he had thought all along that there was something about the Wilkersons that didn't quite add up—and now everything made sense. What puzzled Frank the most now was that he felt guilty every time he gave Agents Martin and Sims details about the Wilkersons. Why? Frank could see in Joe's eyes that he felt the same way.

"Darren left us a note," Joe said. He was trying frantically to think of some way to convey that they knew the Wilkersons were probably headed this way, without giving away that Detective Kitimat was nearby.

"Where is it?" Agent Sims asked excitedly.

"It's back at their house," Joe said. "We had just found it when you guys came."

"We hid because we didn't know who you were," Frank added. "The note's somewhere at the bottom of Darren's closet."

"What did it say?" Agent Martin asked.

"Well, it was written in a hurry, in a secret code that the three of us worked out in Bayport," Joe said, "but it said that his father had just received a coded message on his cell phone that the people who were after them had reached Hudson's Hope and that they needed to leave right away. Darren said they were headed west, through the forest just beyond their house, and were going to a place where nobody would find them."

"That's why we ran this way," Frank said. "We were hoping that we could find their tracks."

Agent Sims looked up at what sky could be seen between the branches of the trees and said, "Well, what are we waiting for? We still have about an hour of light to see by."

Joe picked up his backpack and Frank helped him put it on.

The two FBI agents were dressed for the wilderness, but now Frank realized for the first time that they didn't have anything else with them.

Agent Martin seemed to anticipate what Frank was thinking. "We'll have to share your stuff," he said, "because we left our backpacks back at the Wilkersons' cabin."

"Yeah, we didn't think we'd be chasing you guys so far," Agent Sims added. "We don't have time to go back and get them. We have to find the Wilkersons."

"That's okay. We can share," Joe said. "No problem."

"I could use a swig of water," Agent Martin said.

Frank removed his canteen and handed it to him.

Agent Martin unscrewed the cap, took a big drink, wiped the mouth, put the cap back on, and returned the canteen to Frank. "Thanks," he said.

Frank nodded. He offered the canteen to Agent Sims but he waved it away.

With less light now penetrating to the forest

floor, it was getting harder for them to make their way—but Frank's keen eye had once again picked up the tracks of three people, and Frank was sure it was the Wilkersons. "They're headed in this direction," he said.

Several times they came to rushing streams, made full by the recent rains. Frank knew that the streams had had even more water in them earlier, because the banks were now slick with mud, but they also had deeper tracks of the Wilkersons, which continued to confirm to Frank that they were headed in the right direction.

Occasionally Joe would edge his way next to Frank, asking him as loud as he could to reshift the backpack for him. This also gave Joe a chance to whisper what he was thinking at the moment to Frank.

"For some reason these guys make me nervous," Joe said.

"Me too," Frank agreed with him. "They just took our word that we were friends of the Wilkersons. Wouldn't real agents have asked for our IDs, too?"

Joe nodded. "We need to watch our backs. When I can, I'm going to turn on the walkie-talkie so Detective Kitimat can listen to what's going on."

"Good idea," Frank said.

"Everything all right up there?" Agent Sims called out.

Frank and Joe could tell that the two agents were getting winded. They were keeping up, but barely.

"Yeah—I just needed my pack shifted," Joe called back. "Thanks!"

"What about it, guys?" Agent Martin called. "Are we catching up with the Wilkersons?"

"We sure are," Frank called back. He stopped. "I'll show you." He purposely moved back toward the men and waited for them to catch up.

When the two agents got to where the boys were standing, Frank pointed up ahead and said, "Those are their tracks."

Agent Martin and Agent Sims look carefully at the ground.

"Well, let's don't just stand here," Agent Sims said. "Let's keep going as long as we can still see."

Frank and Joe got back in the lead and started down the trail.

"What was that all about?" Joe whispered.

"Just a little experiment," Frank whispered back. "Those were my tracks."

"Yeah, I know," Joe said. "For a minute, I thought you'd lost your mind."

"Not at all, Joe," Frank said. "We have a big problem here, I think."

"Actually, we have several problems here, Frank," Joe said. "The walkie-talkie must have fallen out of my backpack when that net trap sprung."

"You're kidding me," Frank said.

"I wish I were," Joe said. "But I have an idea."

"Go for it," Frank said.

In his loudest voice, Joe said, "Well, Frank, these tracks are getting hard to see. I hope we don't lose the Wilkersons."

"Hey!" Agent Sims called. "Are you trying to wake the dead?"

Still in a loud voice, Joe shouted, "What? I can't hear you too well. I think I'm allergic to something around here. My ears are all stopped up."

Both FBI agents ran up to them. "Just keep it down," Agent Martin said. "If there's somebody else around besides the Wilkersons, we don't want to let them know we're here."

"Okay!" Joe shouted. "But you'll have to talk really loud if you want me to hear what you're saying."

Agent Martin turned to Frank. "Can't you use sign language with him or something?" he said. "That shouting is getting on my nerves."

Frank nodded. "I think we need to make camp," he said. "Joe's right. It's getting hard to see anything, and if we keep going, we might lose their tracks and never find them again." He waited for a response, but neither agent said anything. "I'm sure the Wilkersons are making camp too," he added, "because they won't be able to see anything either—and I doubt they're using flashlights or anything like that."

"Okay," Agent Martin said.

"Which one of your guys has the tent?" Agent Sims asked.

"Tent?" Joe said. "We were just planning to sleep on the ground."

"No thanks," Agent Martin said. "I'd rather stand."

"Suit yourself," Frank said. He looked around. "Why don't you just lean up against that tree over there?" he said. "It looks pretty comfortable."

Incredibly, the two FBI agents did exactly that, but Frank and Joe spread a couple of branches underneath a tree on the other side of the opening and tried to make themselves as comfortable as possible.

"I don't think our friends are really FBI agents," Frank whispered.

"I agree," Joe said.

"That was a great idea, shouting like you did," Frank said. "Do you think Detective Kitimat heard you?"

Joe shrugged. "I don't know," he said. "I keep hoping that he's out there somewhere, just waiting for the right moment to take those two guys down."

"I think we need to give him a little help, Joe," Frank said.

"How?" Joe asked.

"We should try to escape tomorrow," Frank said.

8 Surrounded

In the morning Joe awoke with a start.

Frank was still asleep, so Joe decided not to disturb him for a couple of minutes. He wanted to think some more about their situation, so that when Frank did finally wake up, he might have a solution to the mess they were in.

He and Frank had stayed awake into the early morning hours, talking about what they needed to do. Agents Sims and Martin—or whoever they really were—both snored so loudly that the Hardys were sure that any forest creatures that might have been curious about these intruders were kept away by the noise.

Neither Joe nor Frank could pinpoint where things had not gone according to plan. First of all, they honestly didn't expect the Wilkersons to be gone. The possibility had entered their minds, of course—but Detective Kitimat's friend hadn't seen the Wilkersons leaving Hudson's Hope in a car. And it had never occurred to him that the Wilkersons would head right into the forest from just beyond their cabin.

That would have been enough of a challenge without the added complication of two men who had initially fooled them into believing they were FBI agents.

"That was really stupid of us," Joe muttered under his breath.

In normal circumstances, he knew, that would never have happened. He and Frank were very familiar with what FBI identification badges looked like and would easily have been able to recognize one that was phony. Of course, when Frank asked to see the men's IDs, Joe knew, he was hanging upside down in a net trap and Frank was wondering if these two guys were going to do something rash. He was probably just so relieved that the men said they were FBI agents that he did no more than give the badges a cursory glance.

Joe wouldn't even be thinking about any of this, of course, if he hadn't stepped into the trap. Normally he was much more cognizant of his surroundings—but when you're being chased through an unfamiliar forest by men brandishing guns, you do tend to be a little less focused than usual, he told himself. The trap was responsible for his losing the walkie-talkie, too, so they couldn't communicate directly with Detective Kitimat.

It was Frank who had figured out why Detective Kitimat probably hadn't shown himself. "I'm sure he overheard these guys say they were FBI agents," he'd said. "That changed the whole dynamic of our situation."

Joe had nodded in agreement. "Especially if he had also heard about this super-secret Witness Protection Program," he said. "He might think that they wouldn't want anyone else to know about it."

"We have to get away from these two guys, Joe, and find the Wilkersons," Frank had said. "My gut tells me I can believe that they're trying to get to this secret location so they can become a part of this special Witness Protection Program that nobody is supposed to know about. But we have to make sure that these two guys don't find them first."

Both Frank and Joe thought that real FBI agents would probably know more about this program than these two did.

Joe could see that the two men were starting to wake up, so he shook Frank's shoulder. "Wake up," he whispered. "I need to tell you something before our phony FBI agents get too close to hear what we're staying."

Frank stifled a yawn. "Okay," he said. "What?"

"Once we're on the trail," Joe said, "we're going to 'accidentally' make life miserable for them."

"How so?" Frank asked.

"We're going to be the worst hikers in the world," Joe whispered. "We're going to let branches go in their faces and we're going to slip and slide whenever we can—but not before we've grabbed hold of one of them to help keep us from falling."

"Sounds like a winning idea," Frank said. He stood up. "Hey, you guys hungry?" he shouted.

"Yes," the two phony agents said. They were standing now, but they still sounded groggy.

Frank tossed them two bags of trail mix, and the two men dug in immediately.

"Is that all you've got?" Agent Sims asked.

"Well, we didn't come prepared for bacon and eggs," Joe said. He stood up. "Sorry."

"We need to be on the trail, anyway," Frank told them. "The Wilkersons will be starting out soon too, and we don't want them to get too far ahead."

"We actually need to move faster than they do," Joe added. "It's really a simple law of physics."

"Huh?" Agent Martin said. "What's that got to do with anything?"

"If we walk at the same speed they're walking, we'll never reach them," Frank explained. "We have to walk faster than they do."

"Oh, yeah," Agent Sims said. "Well, what are we waiting for?"

The Hardys put on their backpacks.

"Actually, we're waiting for you guys," Joe said. He grinned at them. "Ready?"

Frank could tell that both agents wanted to make a smart retort, but they didn't. Instead they walked across the clearing and got behind Frank and Joe.

"Show me their tracks again," Agent Martin said after they had been walking for about fifteen minutes. "You guys aren't trying to get us lost, are you?"

Joe hadn't been prepared for that question. Up until now, he had honestly felt that the two phony FBI agents believed everything they had said.

The Hardys stopped.

"There they are," Joe said. He pointed to the tracks—he was sure they were from the Wilkersons.

"Okay," Agent Sims said. "We were just checking."

"That was a dumb thing to say," Frank told him. "Why would we try to get us lost?"

"Yeah," Joe added. "We're planning to join the Wilkersons ourselves and go where they go."

"You don't think anybody will try to stop us, do you?" Frank asked. "After all, we're not running from any criminals, like the Wilkersons are."

Agent Sims shook his head. "Naw, it won't be a problem," he said—a bit quickly, Joe thought. "They won't mind if you want to spend the rest of your lives there."

"Yeah, it's just up to you," Agent Martin added. "I

hear there are a lot of people there who've just dropped out of society."

"That's good to hear," Frank said. "That's what my brother and I are planning to do."

"Come on. We're wasting too much time," Joe said. He picked up his pace to a fast walk. "We'll never find them if we have to keep stopping to explain all of this to you guys."

Just then, Frank and Joe had to part a couple of low hanging branches in order to stay on the trail. In unison, they let the branches go as the phony agents came even with them.

The two men let out loud, ear-piercing howls and immediatley grabbed their faces.

"Hey! Watch it!" Agent Martin screamed. "Are you two crazy or something?"

"What happened?" Frank cried. "Are you two all right?"

"No, we're *not* all right," Agent Sims said. "My face is on fire!"

"Oh, I'm so sorry," Frank said in as innocent a voice as he could muster. "I honestly didn't know you were that close behind me."

Joe could see huge red welts on the faces of both men. He knew just by looking that it must have been really painful.

"There's probably a stream up ahead," Frank said. "You can put some cold water on your faces. That'll help."

"Well come on, then," Agent Martin said. "I've never had anything hurt me this much."

The two phony FBI agents were now walking side by side with the Hardys, looking ahead expectantly for the water that Frank had promised them.

It was another fifteen minutes before Frank heard the rush of a mountain stream. "It won't be long now," he said.

Joe was almost feeling sorry for the two agents, because the welts on their faces had swollen considerably. Still, when they reached the stream, which was wider than he thought it would be, he decided that it was time to create another problem for Agents Sims and Martin.

As Agent Martin gingerly stepped out onto the rocks at the side of the rushing water, Joe followed him closely, and, just as Agent Martin leaned over to scoop up a handful of the cold water, Joe pretended to slip, shouted, "Don't let me fall!", and knocked Agent Martin into the middle of the cold water.

"AAAAAGGGGHHHH!" Agent Martin screamed.

Frank and Agent Sims rushed to the bank.

"Oh, I'm so sorry," Joe said. "I was about to fall, and I thought I could keep from doing it by holding on to Agent Martin."

"I saw the whole thing," Frank said quickly. "That's exactly what happened."

"You clumsy idiot!" Agent Sims screamed. He

was stretched out on the muddy bank, reaching his arm out to Agent Martin, who now was standing in the middle of the frigid rushing mountain water. "Grab hold, Jersey!" Agent Sims shouted.

"I'm trying, Willy!" Agent Martin shouted.

Frank looked at Joe. *Jersey? Willy?* he mouthed and rolled his eyes.

Finally Agent Martin was able to reach Agent Sims's hand so he could be pulled out of the water.

Joe was prepared for an onslaught of angry words, but Agent Martin was shivering so much that he was unable to get anything out of his mouth.

"Should we build a fire and let him dry off?" Frank suggested.

"No!" Agent Sims said, baring his teeth. "He'll dry off while we're running through the forest."

"Okay," Frank said. "Let's walk down this way. There may be a narrower place to cross."

Frank had already seen that this was exactly what the Wilkersons had done, because the tracks led in the direction he was now headed—but it hadn't seemed to occur to the two phony FBI agents to ask about that. The only thing that seemed to be on Agent Martin's mind was staying warm. From time to time, they came into sunlight, and Joe noticed that Agent Martin slowed down—but Agent Sims would always gruffly tell him to speed up.

Gradually Frank and Joe edged far enough ahead

of the two men that they could whisper to each other without being heard.

"The Wilkersons must not have crossed the stream, because their tracks are moving away from it now, heading toward that ravine over there," Frank said. "I don't think they're too far away, either."

"Then I think it's time we make our move," Joe said.

"The problem is, how are we going to do it so that they don't immediately know what has happened?" Frank said. He stopped and glanced back at the two men. "You two all right?" he shouted.

"Yeah, keep going," Agent Sims shouted back. "Don't worry about us."

"That's what we're planning on doing," Joe muttered. "That's *exactly* what we're planning on doing."

"I think I know how we can do it, because that brush up ahead is really thick," Frank said. "It'll be easy to get lost."

"Yeah," Joe agreed. "It'll take them a while to realize that we're gone."

Frank and Joe started walking a little faster, but not so fast that the two men would notice. When they reached the thick underbrush, they plunged through it, glad that their clothing—for the most part—would protect them from getting badly scratched. Then they sped up.

When Frank thought they were far enough into

the brush that they couldn't be seen, they started down the side of the steep ravine.

"Are we going to lose the Wilkersons' trail, Frank?" Joe asked.

"No," Frank said. "Right before they reached this underbrush, they veered to the right. I saw the broken grass, but I don't think those two bozos will notice it. They'll just plunge into this brush after us."

"You're sure we can find their tracks again?" Joe said.

"I'm positive," Frank said. "We'll cross this ravine, but those guys will stay on this side of it."

The going was rough because they had to contend with the thick tangles of vines and branches and the steep plunge of the side of the ravine—but finally they reached the bottom. They found that the floor was full of water, but not so much that it was impossible to cross.

Immediately they crossed over and began climbing up the other side of the ravine. Finally they reached the top.

"Now we just need to make our way out of this underbrush, and we'll be back on the Wilkersons' trail," Frank said.

Another fifty feet and they were onto more manageable terrain.

"That's amazing," Joe said. "I would have thought this was almost impenetrable."

"It looks that way," Frank agreed. He had stopped

and was searching the ground. Finally he said, "There they are."

"Those tracking classes you took at the national park last year have really paid off, haven't they?" Joe said.

"You got that right," Frank said. "Come on!"

They picked up their pace, following the Wilkersons' tracks—then Frank stopped. "Oh, no!" he said.

"What's wrong?" Joe asked.

"Look!" Frank said. He pointed to the ground. "These tracks are doubling back on us now."

"What does that mean?" Joe said.

"It probably means that the Wilkersons didn't continue on in this direction, because the terrain got too rough," Frank said. He looked around. "They're going back toward the ravine."

"So they crossed over and then returned?" Joe asked.

"That's what I'm afraid of," Frank said. He took a pair of binoculars out of his backpack. "There's a spot just a few feet back where we can see across the ravine," he said. "I want to find out what's going on over there."

The Hardy boys backtracked. When they reached the spot that Frank had mentioned, they stopped.

Frank scanned the top of the cliff with the binoculars. "Oh, no!" he said. "I can't believe this."

"Let me see," Joe said.

Frank handed him the binoculars. Joe could clearly see Mr. and Mrs. Wilkerson and Darren, dressed for hiking, with large packs on their backs. Moving the binoculars to his left, he could also see the two phony FBI agents. They were out of the heavy brush and were at the edge of the ravine too. And the two groups were heading right toward each other.

"We have to warn them!" Frank said.

Joe was just about to shout a warning across the ravine to the Wilkersons when they were suddenly surrounded by two armed men.

9 The New Plan

Everything happened so fast that neither Frank nor Joe had time to register exactly what was going on—and then a third man appeared.

"Detective Kitimat!" Frank said. He looked at the two other men. "Who are these guys?"

"These are Agents Martin and Sims out of the Seattle, Washington, FBI office," Detective Kitimat said as he pointed out each man. "We sort of ran into each other on the trail. I've known these two men for a long time."

"What?" Frank and Joe said in unison. "You've got to be kidding!"

"What do you mean?" Agent Sims said.

"Could we see your identification, please?" Frank said.

Joe could tell that the two men thought this was a waste of time, but they didn't say so and they quickly produced their FBI identification.

This time, both Frank and Joe scrutinized the badges very carefully.

"Well, I guess you really are who you say you are," Frank said.

"Unlike that other Agent Martin and Agent Sims," Joe added.

"Now what are *you* talking about?" Agent Martin asked.

Frank quickly told them the entire story of what had happened with the two phony FBI agents, from the time he and Joe encountered them in the Wilkersons' cabin, to when they had escaped.

Agent Martin and Agent Sims looked at each other.

"The fact that they knew exactly who'd be coming for the Wilkersons means there's a leak somewhere in this chain of command—and it explains a lot about what happened to us," Agent Sims said. "We'll have to find the leak quick and get it plugged."

"What do you mean?" Frank asked. "How'd they get to the Wilkersons' cabin before you guys?"

"We were driving into Hudson's Hope when we were pulled over by the British Columbia Provincial Police," Agent Martin said. "The whole thing's smelled fishy from the very beginning, but we thought that maybe somebody out of Hudson's Hope just didn't get the message."

"It's happened before," Agent Sims added. "Most of the time the law enforcement agencies of our two countries work very well together, but sometimes you have people in these little towns who get territorial and do everything they can to stymie your investigations."

"They resent their own country's agencies that are above them," Agent Martin said, "and when you're not even a member of a police force in their country, you can really run into a brick wall."

"This particular officer had been 'tipped off' by someone," Agent Sims said. "He kept telling us that some American FBI agents were coming into town, planning to take Canadian law into their own hands."

"We're working with the British Columbia authorities on this case," Agent Martin told them. "We kept showing him the papers, but he wouldn't listen."

"Finally we convinced him to call a number in Victoria, and he did," Agent Sims said. "Then he apologized, more or less—but of course by then we had been delayed enough that the Wilkersons were already gone when we got to their cabin."

"But we could tell by the tracks leading away from the cabin that several people had headed into the woods," Agent Martin said, "so we immediately started after them."

"They found me," Detective Kitimat said, "and then we found you two."

"This whole thing is getting more and more bizarre," Joe said. "Those two phony FBI agents kept talking about an ultra-secret Witness Protection Program that very few people know about."

Frank could tell that the two FBI agents were stunned by what they had just heard. "Are they right?" he asked them point blank.

"Look," Agent Martin said, obviously frustrated by the turn of events, "we need to find the Wilkersons, and we think they're around here somewhere. Can this explanation just wait until then?"

"Well, Frank and I can tell you exactly where the Wilkersons are," Joe said. He turned and pointed across the ravine. "They're over there, on the other side."

"Then what are we waiting for?" Agent Sims said. "Let's cross over."

Agents Martin and Sims started walking toward the edge of the ravine.

"Uh, there's just a slight problem," Joe said without moving. "You see, by now the Wilkersons are probably in the hands of those two *phony* FBI agents. We saw them headed in that direction right before you reached us. In fact we had just started to shout a warning to them."

"It may be too late for them now," Frank said. He took his binoculars and scanned the top of the opposite side of the ravine. "Those two phony FBI agents may have decided to do away with them."

"Not a chance," Agent Martin said. "They need the Wilkersons."

"You're right. They're all talking to each other," Frank said, surprise in his voice. "In fact the Wilkersons look almost glad to see them." He lowered the binoculars. "Well, I have to admit that their IDs fooled me, too. They must have also convinced the Wilkersons that they're FBI agents." Frank handed the binoculars to Joe. "We thought those two guys must be looking for the Wilkersons so they could hurt them—but now they're all acting like they're the best of friends. What's going on here?"

"They're after bigger fish," Agent Sims said.

"Bigger Fish?" Joe said.

Agent Martin nodded. "Oh, I have no doubt that they eventually plan to do away with all three of the Wilkersons," he said, "but that's only after they get to Hidden Mountain so they can also get rid of some of the other people who live there."

"Hidden Mountain," Frank said. "That's the name of this secret Witness Protection Program?"

Agent Sims nodded. "But we can't let that happen," he said. "We have to make sure the Wilkersons get there safely—but we can't allow those two thugs to get anywhere near it."

"May I?" Agent Martin asked, indicating that he'd like to borrow the binoculars.

Joe handed them to him. "Sure," he said.

Agent Martin adjusted the binoculars and scanned the top of the ravine. "Mr. Wilkerson is pointing north," he said. "I think they're ready to be on their way again."

Detective Kitimat had been quiet until that moment. "So what's the plan?" he asked. "Do I hold back and shadow the four of you, or what?"

"I think we need to stay together until we can figure out a way to separate the Wilkersons from those two guys without *spooking* the Wilkersons," Agent Martin said. "Unfortunately for us, they were probably so willing to believe those guys were who they said they were that it would be difficult for us to gain their trust right now."

Agent Sims looked at Frank and Joe. "Detective Kitimat told us what your original plan was," he said, "and I think it still has some merit."

"I agree," Agent Martin said. "We have to somehow let the Wilkersons see you two so they'll know right away they can trust us—but make sure that the two phony agents aren't aware of what's happening."

"I understand," Frank said. "If the two phony FBI agents know we're with *real* FBI agents, they'll cut their losses by doing away with the Wilkersons and trying to escape."

"Exactly," Agent Sims said.

"We should get started, then," Detective Kitimat said. "We still have to cross that ravine before we can start trailing them, and that's going to take a while."

"Agreed," Agents Martin and Sims said.

The five of them started the descent on their side of the ravine. Joe was surprised at how adept the two real FBI men were at this. He should have caught on right away that there was something wrong with the phony agents, instead of trying to make excuses for them. The FBI wouldn't send agents into such a rugged area as this without giving them some kind of wilderness training.

When they reached the bottom of the ravine, Agent Martin started walking alongside Frank and Joe.

"We know your father," he told them. "Because of that we have no problem letting you know what we're up against."

"We appreciate that," Joe said. "We've been taught how to keep secrets."

Agent Martin nodded. "I'm sure you have. Well, from what you said, those two phony agents didn't mention the words Hidden Mountain exactly, right?"

"No, they didn't," Frank said.

"That's very important to know," Agent Martin continued. "We've been aware for some time that certain criminal elements suspected that a secret Witness Protection Program existed, but we hoped that none of them knew the name."

"Well, I can't speak for what the other criminal

elements you're talking about know," Joe said, "but I can guarantee you that those two phony agents never once mentioned the words 'Hidden Mountain.'"

"Do the Wilkersons know the name?" Frank asked. "Because if they do, and if they think these two agents are the real thing, then they'll probably tell them."

"That won't really matter," Agent Martin said, "because our job is to make sure that these two phony agents never make it back to civilization."

10 Bear Attack

At Frank's suggestion, the boys took the lead in the climb up the opposite side of the ravine.

"The Wilkersons were expecting a couple of FBI agents, so they weren't spooked by those two guys," Frank said, "but they're not expecting anybody else. If for some reason they happened to see all of us together, they might panic—and then there's no telling what those two guys would do . . . to them *and* to us."

Agents Martin and Sims agreed that made sense.

Even on the outside, Joe could tell the difference between the two real FBI men and the two phony FBI men. The real agents were in great physical shape and could easily keep up with them. He remembered how out of shape the other two guys were.

As they neared the top of the ravine, Frank and Joe motioned for the agents and Detective Kitimat to stop.

Slowly Joe raised his head to eye level with the ground, saw that nobody was around, and stood up. He motioned everyone else on to the top.

"This is about where the Wilkersons met up with the two phony agents," Frank said, "so now what we need to do is find where they restarted their trip toward Hidden Mountain."

With the five of them searching, it wasn't long before they found the tracks of the Wilkersons and the two phony FBI agents.

"Let's go!" Frank said.

As stealthily as possible, he and Joe led the way through the forest, both of them remembering a summer several years ago when George Long Bow, a Kiowa lawyer from Lawton, Oklahoma, and a very good friend of their father's, had taught them how his ancestors had silently tracked wild game in the nearby Wichita Mountains.

Once, when they came to a small meadow, Joe looked up and saw a golden eagle soaring high above them, effortlessly riding the air currents—perhaps setting its sights on a small animal huddled between two boulders.

Detective Kitimat hurried up to them, impressing

both the Hardy boys with his easy breathing. "How far ahead of us do you think they are?" he asked.

"A mile, maybe two," Frank said. "That's just an estimate, of course."

"You can see where the grass has been trampled," Joe added, "but it's beginning to right itself, so that means some time has passed."

Detective Kitimat nodded. "Good work, boys," he said, and dropped back with Agents Martin and Sims.

Another hour passed before the Hardy boys slowed their pace.

"We're getting close enough to them now that I think we need to talk about our next step," Frank said.

"Okay," Joe said. He pointed up ahead. "That looks like a good place to stop. I think I hear water, too."

Frank and Joe stopped and waited for Agents Martin and Sims and Detective Kitimat to reach them.

"We've kept up a pretty good pace," Frank said. "We were probably going twice as fast as the Wilkersons and the two phony agents."

"The bent grass here is closer to the ground," Joe said. "They're not too far ahead of us."

"We need to stop and go over some final details," Frank said. "We have to be sure that our plan of attack is foolproof."

"I agree," Agent Martin said.

The place Joe had suggested they stop turned

out to be almost like a manicured park in the middle of the wilderness.

Agent Sims sat down and leaned up against a tree trunk. "Man! I have to tell you something, guys," he said, addressing Frank and Joe. "You two are in *really* good shape."

"That's for sure," Agent Martin said, sitting next to Agent Sims. "You're making us look bad."

"Whatever training you receive at Bayport High School, they should institute at Quantico," Agent Sims said. "You guys don't even seem to be out of breath."

Frank and Joe grinned.

"Well, we *do* put in a lot of hours training," Joe said, "and we're a few years younger than you guys."

"Touché," Agent Sims said.

"Hey, guys, look over here!" Detective Kitimat said. He was standing at the opposite edge of the clearing.

The Hardy boys and the two FBI agents walked over to him.

"What's wrong?" Joe said.

Detective Kitimat pointed. "The branches of that berry bush were just recently pulled down by bears," he said, "and they dug up those anthills over there, too."

"Are you telling me that we've got bears nearby?" Agent Sims said.

Detective Kitimat nodded. "We met a mother and her cubs on the way in," he said.

"Actually, we wouldn't even be here now," Joe said, "if a chipmunk hadn't saved our lives."

The two FBI agents gave him a peculiar look, but they didn't ask him to explain.

"I think this means that we need to hurry up, make our plans, and get back on the trail," Detective Kitimat said.

Joe thought he seemed nervous about it.

"What I'm thinking is this," Frank said. "By now those two phony agents may be dragging far enough behind the Wilkersons that Joe and I can intercept the Wilkersons and cut them off long enough from the two guys so that the three of you can capture them."

Agent Martin and Sims nodded.

"I think that might work," Agent Martin said, "but you need to make sure that they take cover right away, because those two guys wouldn't hesitate to start shooting as soon as they realized what was happening."

"Maybe Frank and I can confront Darren on the trail, then use him to get his mom and dad off the trail and into the heavy underbrush before the two phony agents realize what happened," Joe said. "I don't think they're expecting anything like this." As he finished, he took a swipe at a cloud of mosquitoes that had begun swarming around his head.

"Well, it's the only plan we have—but it's a good plan," Agent Sims said, "so let's go with it."

With Frank and Joe once again in the lead, they started back through the forest. Within a mile, though, it opened up into a narrow meadow laced with streams trickling through it.

"Let me see the binoculars, Joe," Frank said.

Joe handed them to him and Frank adjusted the lenses to his eyes. "Bingo!" he said. "There they are. On the other side of the meadow."

"What is it?" Detective Kitimat asked as he and the two agents came up behind Frank and Joe.

Frank handed Agent Martin the binoculars. "Those two guys don't seem to be having any trouble keeping up," he said.

"That's what I was thinking," Frank told them.

"What now?" Agent Sims said. "It'll be hard to separate them if they stay that close."

"I know," Frank said, disappointment in his voice.

"Well, we need to keep walking," Agent Martin said, "because they're not stopping."

"We should skirt the meadow just inside the tree line," Joe said. "They won't see us that way."

They all agreed that Joe was right.

The Hardy boys led them three trees deep into the woods that bordered the meadow and started after the Wilkersons. Once again they paced themselves at twice the speed they thought the Wilkersons and the two phony agents would be walking—so it wasn't long until they had covered the length of the meadow and started looking once again for the Wilkersons' tracks.

For the next two hours, no one spoke, afraid that the sound might carry. Finally Frank lifted a hand and motioned everyone toward him and Joe.

"They're staying together," he whispered. "It has to be the adrenaline from knowing they're so near to Hidden Mountain and to finding all the people they want to get rid of."

"That would be in character with members of the crime syndicate," Agent Martin said. "We may have to rethink our plans and rush them."

"It'll be dark soon, so they'll be stopping for the night," Joe said. "Let's see what kind of new plan we can come up with over the next few hours."

"Okay," Agent Sims said. "You know the Wilkersons better than we do."

"I'm not so sure," Frank admitted. "We thought we did. We weren't prepared for this."

"I really don't think Darren knew about any of this," Joe said. "I think he's our hope. We just have to figure out how to involve him in solving this problem."

In another hour it had gotten too dark for them to see. "We have to stop here," Frank said. "We may come upon them without warning if we don't and then there's no telling what'll happen."

"Hey, do you see that?" Joe whispered.

"What?" Frank said.

Joe was moving his head around in the direction of the trail they had been following. "I'm sure it was a pinpoint of light."

"Fireflies," Detective Kitimat said.

"No, I don't think it was," Joe said. "It was a little larger than a . . . there! Look!"

Everyone strained to see what Joe was pointing at.

"It's a campfire," Detective Kitimat said. "I'm sure it is."

"That makes sense," Frank said. "They don't have any reason to suspect that we're here, so why not have a small fire?"

"That's good news," Agent Martin said. "You don't make fires if you're suspicious of anything."

"Well, I say we set up camp too, minus the fire, of course," Agent Sims said. "We know where they are, and I'm sure they're not going to go anywhere until morning."

Frank, Joe, and Detective Kitimat dropped their gear onto the ground where they were.

"I want to keep an eye on that fire," Frank said.

"We'll set up camp back down the trail," Agent Martin said. "There's a nice patch of grass that I think has my name on it."

Frank and Joe found some soft ferns, broke off as many fronds as they could, and made soft beds for themselves and Detective Kitimat.

"Wow!" Joe said as he stretched out on the ferns. "Is this really as comfortable as I think it is, or have

I just been away from my soft bed too long?"

"Probably a little of both," Detective Kitimat said. "But there's nothing like a bed of ferns when you're really tired."

Frank let out a big yawn. "You're telling me," he said. "Joe, why don't you take first watch, okay?"

"Thanks a lot, Frank," Joe said. "Why did you wait until I was all comfortable to ask me?"

"Why don't you two let me take first watch?" Detective Kitimat said. "I'm actually too keyed-up to sleep."

"You sure you don't mind?" Frank said.

"Really, I was just kidding Frank," Joe told Detective Kitimat. "I don't mind."

"No, I really want to," Detective Kitimat said. "Get some sleep. I think a lot is going to happen tomorrow."

The boys both yawned. "Okay," they said sleepily.

Frank opened his eyes. Someone was shaking his shoulder.

"Frank! Frank! Wake up!" a voice whispered in his ear. It was Detective Kitimat. "There's something wrong."

Frank woke immediately, and his movement awakened Joe.

"What's wrong?" Joe asked.

"Don't say anything," Detective Kitimat said. "I think we've got trouble."

At that moment, down the trail—from the direction where the two FBI agents were sleeping—there was low growl, then a human groan.

Suddenly a voice said, "No! No!" It was followed by something that sounded like a whacking noise.

Immediately the Hardy boys and Detective Kitimat were on their feet.

Frank shone a penlight in the direction of the noise. A huge brown bear was reared up on its hind legs. Suddenly there was a popping sound, and the bear fell to the ground.

The boys and Detective Kitimat rushed to where the bear was—and what they discovered was something out of a nightmare.

Agent Martin was leaning up against a tree, a dart gun in one hand. He was covered with blood. Beyond him Agent Sims was lying on the ground. He wasn't moving.

"You check out Agent Martin," Detective Kitimat said. "I'll check on Agent Sims."

"What happened?" Joe said when they reached Agent Martin. It was a dumb question, he knew, because it was obvious that the bear had attacked them both.

"Don't worry about me," Agent Martin said. "It's Agent Sims who's in bad shape."

"Detective Kitimat is taking care of him," Frank said. "We're here to take care of you."

"I'm sure I look worse than I am," Agent Martin

said. "The bear managed to slap at me a couple of time before I was able to get the tranquilizer gun out of my gear and shoot him."

"Tranquilizer gun?" Joe said.

"Yeah. We have strict instructions regarding the wildlife up here," Agent Martin said. "We can't kill any of it." He pointed to the bear. "You guys are safe. She'll be out for almost twenty-four hours, but she'll be all right when she finally wakes up."

"Really?" Frank said.

Agent Martin winced and nodded. "The FBI developed a special tranquilizer just for situations like this," he said. "It puts bears into a twenty-four-hour hibernation."

"I've done all I can for Agent Sims," Detective Kitimat said. "He's pretty badly mauled, and he needs medical attention right away."

With the Hardy boys' help, Agent Martin stood up. "Help me make a stretcher out of some of those stronger branches," he said. "I'll pull him back down the trail until we're far enough away that a helicopter won't be heard by our friends up there."

"We'll go with you," Joe said.

"No, you won't," Agent Martin said. "We're prepared for this."

"What do you mean?" Frank asked.

"This mission has to be carried out," Agent Martin said. "It's up to the three of you to make sure it is."

Frank and Joe looked at each other and then at Detective Kitimat.

"We can do it," Frank assured Agent Martin. "We'll make sure the Wilkersons get to Hidden Mountain, and we'll make sure that the phony FBI agents don't."

Agent Martin handed Frank an envelope. "If you aren't able to separate them before you reach Hidden Mountain, then you're to open this envelope and follow the instructions."

11 Saving the Wilkersons

Using branches, Frank, Joe, and Detective Kitimat were able to put together a strong stretcher. They knew it would hold Agent Sims while Agent Martin pulled him far enough back through the forest that Agent Martin could radio for a helicopter and not be heard by the Wilkersons or the two phony FBI agents.

"This thing is amazing," Agent Martin said as they all helped lift Agent Sims onto it. "How did you do it?"

"Native Americans used to use these when they were traveling too," Joe told him. "Frank and I spent a summer learning how to make them."

"You learned well," Agent Martin said.

"Thanks," the Hardys said.

Frank and Joe loaded Agent Sims's equipment onto the end of the bearer, then helped Agent Martin fasten himself to the front, so that he'd be using his body to pull it.

"I know this mission is in good hands," Agent Martin said. "I'm sure it'll come to a successful conclusion."

"We won't let you down," Joe told him.

"When you've captured those two phony agents, just radio in the helicopter using this number." Agent Martin handed Detective Kitimat a piece of paper. "Our men are waiting at the airport in Dawson Creek and are ready to pick those two guys up."

Frank noticed that Agent Martin didn't mention the envelope again. *He's probably hoping we won't have to use the instructions inside,* he decided.

Within minutes Agent Martin was pulling his load back down the trail. The Hardys and Detective Kitimat waited until they could no longer hear them, then they returned to where they had left their gear and sat down.

"We should probably try to get some sleep," Detective Kitimat said, "but I'm wide awake and still a little nervous about that bear."

"So am I," Joe said. "What if that tranquilizer doesn't work?"

"Well, while we're waiting to see, I suggest that we finalize our plans to separate the phony agents from the Wilkersons," Frank said. Joe nodded.

For the next several minutes, they all sat together, mulling over all kinds of possible scenarios for what would take place in the next few hours.

Finally Joe said, "I don't see any other option except to rejoin those two phony FBI agents and pretend that we've been lost all this time, trying to find them."

"That was what I was thinking too," Frank said. "I've racked my brain and can't come up with any other great ideas."

Detective Kitimat didn't say anything, but the boys could tell that he wasn't quite sure that was a good idea.

"We'll be careful," Joe told him. "Frank and I are pretty good actors."

"I just thought of something, Joe," Frank said. "If we could get to Darren while they're all asleep and tell him what's going on, he could relay that to his parents. Then you and I could just pretend that we stumbled onto their camp and take it from there."

"That might work better, Frank," Joe said. "That way we'd have the Wilkersons in on the plan right away."

"That's what I was thinking," Frank said.

Detective Kitimat nodded. "I think that sounds much better. If, as you said, you don't think those two phony FBI agents have any inkling that they're being followed, then you just might be able to pull it off," he said. "If you're in camp with them, you'll have a much better chance of separating them from the Wilkersons—then I can capture them and call in the FBI."

"We've got to keep them from reaching Hidden Mountain," Joe said. "This is the only way I think we can do that."

Joe looked at his watch. "We have about three hours until dawn," he said. "We should get started right away."

"I agree," Frank said.

The three of them stood up, put on their back-packs, and headed back down the trail toward where the boys were sure the Wilkersons and the phony FBI agents had stopped for the night.

"We'll have to use this penlight," Frank said. "We can't see without it."

"We'll just have to hope that they think they're home free and are not concerned that anybody else is in the woods," Joe said. Suddenly he stopped. "I hadn't really thought about this, Frank. I wonder what they think happened to us. They may be worried that we'll show up."

"I think I read them right, Joe," Frank said. "Those two aren't concerned about anybody but themselves."

"They probably think you two are lost in the wilderness and have been eaten by bears by now," Detective Kitimat said. "From your description of them, they don't sound too bright."

"They're not," Joe said.

For the next hour they used the penlight to help them see their way through the forest. Just as they got to the edge of the clearing of the camp, Frank turned it off.

"Well, I guess this is where we leave you," he said to Detective Kitimat. "I wish I hadn't lost that walkie-talkie when I sprung that net trap."

"Don't worry about it, Joe," Detective Kitimat said. "I don't plan to be so far away from you that I won't be able to hear loud talking."

"That sounds like a good idea," Frank told him.

He and Joe headed to their left so they could skirt the small clearing where the Wilkersons and the two phony agents were spending the night. Within minutes they could see into their camp—but it wasn't what they were expecting.

The clearing wasn't as large as the Hardy boys had hoped it would be. The Wilkersons were sleeping under the overhang of a large outcropping of rock. The two phony FBI agents had positioned themselves so that if the Wilkersons tried to walk into the clearing, they'd have to pass by one of the men.

"Clever," Joe said. "These two guys may be smarter than we gave them credit for."

"Agreed," Frank whispered. "They probably told the Wilkersons that they could have the protected sleeping spaces, while they stayed out in the open— when the whole time, there was a reason for it."

"Yeah. They're not going to take a chance on the Wilkersons suddenly thinking they're not on the up-and-up and trying to get away," Joe said. "How are we going to implement this plan now?"

"Well, I think this is a good time to try out that rope we bought for mountain climbing," Frank said. "We should be able to rappel down that outcropping of rock right beside where Darren is sleeping, wake him up, and tell him what's going on. He can then relay the information to his parents. After that we can pretend that we just walked into the camp, saw everybody was there, and went right to sleep so we wouldn't wake them up—and that we planned to explain everything in the morning."

Joe mulled over what he had just heard. "Well, it's just crazy enough to work," he agreed.

Slowly the Hardy boys worked their way up the other side of the clearing. The rocks had only been exposed in the clearing, probably due to some centuries-old flood, Frank thought. Back in the forest itself, the rocks were still under the soil. When Frank and Joe reached the summit, they had a bird's-eye view of the clearing below.

"This should be a piece of cake," Joe said. "We've got enough rope that we can loop it around one of the trunks of these trees, go down the rocks using the two ropes, and then pull it down with us after we're on the ground."

"Exactly," Frank said. "There's no way those

two phony agents will know how we got there."

Joe looped the rope around the closest tree to the side of the outcropping, evened it out, then, holding onto both ropes, he started down the side of the rocks.

When Joe was down a few feet, Frank grabbed hold of the ropes and started down after Joe.

The rope was long enough that when Joe reached the end of it, he was only about a foot off the ground. He jumped the rest of the way and landed soundlessly on the soft grass just outside the overhang—about two feet from where Darren was sleeping.

Joe looked up and saw Frank slowly working his way down the side of the rocks. He hadn't realized how much the campfire lit up the area. Frank was visible to anyone who might happen to look up. Joe held his breath.

Finally Frank made it down far enough that he could jump, then Joe took hold of one of the ropes and slowly began pulling it down toward them. It caught in a sharp rock, but Joe didn't want to jerk it, thinking that it might send one of the rocks down on the sleeping Wilkersons. Finally, by shaking out the rope, he was able to get it loose. When he had the complete rope in his hands, he wound it up and put it back in his pack.

"Now let's go let Darren in on what's happening," Frank whispered.

The Hardys got as close to Darren as they could before Frank started shaking his shoulders.

Darren finally opened his eyes. When he saw the Hardy boys standing over him, he opened his mouth—but Joe immediately clamped a hand over it.

"Don't say anything, Darren" Joe whispered. "Just listen carefully. Okay?"

Darren nodded.

Frank quickly told him that the two men in camp with them were phony FBI agents, and he and Joe were there to make sure the Wilkersons made it to Hidden Mountain.

"We're going to try to separate the two men from you and your family," Joe added. "We have a detective friend of our father's nearby, ready to take them into custody."

"But we have to work this just right so we don't jeopardize your family," Frank said.

"I understand," Darren whispered. "It sure is great to see you two."

"It's great to see you too, Darren!" Frank whispered.

"Now, we need you to tell your parents what's going on," Joe said. "But hurry, because those men might wake up any minute. We're going to sneak out, so it'll look like we just stumbled onto you guys while you were sleeping and rejoined the trip to the location of the ultra-secret Witness Protection Program."

"Are you sure they'll believe you?" Darren whispered.

Frank shrugged. "I guess we'll find out in the morning," he said.

The Hardys made themselves comfortable just outside the overhang. They watched as Darren crawled over to his parents, woke them, and whispered what Frank and Joe had just told him.

After a few minutes Darren crawled back over to where the Hardy boys were lying.

"Dad was already starting to think that something was wrong, but he didn't know what to do about it," Darren told them. "He trusts you two now, and he's glad you've come."

"What do you mean 'now'?" Frank asked.

"He's the one who cut me off when I was talking over the shortwave radio," Darren explained. "It was in the cabin when we rented it, and the owner said we could listen to it, but that we couldn't call out because we weren't licensed. I called out anyway, though, hoping I'd reach you guys."

"You did," Joe said. "That's why we're here."

"Dad unplugged it right in the middle of my message, because he didn't trust anybody," Darren said.

"We didn't see a shortwave radio in the cabin," Frank said. "What happened to it?"

"Dad locked it up in a shed behind the cabin," Darren said.

Just then one of the phony FBI agents stirred. When it looked as though he wasn't going to wake up, Darren said, "See you in the morning."

The sun woke Joe. When he opened his eyes, both phony FBI agents—Willy and Jersey—were standing over him and Frank, looking completely puzzled.

"Hey, guys! We thought we'd never find you!" Joe said. He sat up and yawned. "We looked everywhere."

"Why'd you run off?" Jersey demanded.

By now, Frank was awake. "We didn't run off," he said sleepily. "We got lost, and then a bear chased us for miles."

Willy laughed.

"It wasn't funny," Joe said. "We could have been killed."

"Mom, Dad! It's Frank and Joe!" Darren shouted. "Hey, guys! You've come to join us after all."

"Yeah!" Joe shouted over to him. "We told you we were planning to run away from home!"

"This is cool!" Frank said. "We're going to live the rest of our lives in the wilderness."

The two phony FBI agents looked at each other and shrugged. Joe could tell that they were unsure what to do next.

"Everybody up!" Jersey shouted. "There are people waiting for us at Hidden Mountain."

The Hardys looked at each other. They had

been right. When the Wilkersons first encountered the two phony FBI agents, they were probably so glad to see them that they told them
everything. It was only afterward that they had
begun suspecting something was wrong.

Jersey was looking at a piece of paper.

"What's that?" Joe asked, looking over his shoulder.

"It's the map to Hidden Mountain," he said. He
grinned at Joe. "Mr. Wilkerson had it. I told him
that it might be better if I kept it, since we were
supposed to make sure they made it there safely."
The man's look gave Joe chills.

"That's a good idea," Joe said, unconvincingly.

Joe hurried over to where Frank was repacking
their gear. "I don't know if they really believe us or
not," he said, "but they probably won't try anything
in front of the Wilkersons."

"Probably not," Frank said, "but we need to watch
our backs because I wouldn't put it past them to set
up some kind of accident for us."

"Yeah," Joe said. He suddenly wondered just how
much longer he and Frank would be able to stay
alive.

12 Danger on the Trail

While Willy and Jersey were arguing about their gear and who was to carry what, and Mrs. Wilkerson and Darren were busy putting out the campfire, Mr. Wilkerson managed to maneuver himself close enough to Frank and Joe that he was able to explain some of what had transpired since they had left Bayport.

A government agent had come to the Wilkersons' house one night, disguised as a door-to-door salesman, and he'd told them that they had to leave that night. He'd said that the crime syndicate figures who had been after them for years had finally traced them to Bayport, and since this was their fourth relocation, the United States government required them to go into the ultra-secret Witness Protection

Program if they wanted further protection. That would mean relocating to Hidden Mountain, in the northern part of British Columbia. Mr. Wilkerson explained that the government shared the location with the Canadian government.

"He told us that once we're there, though, we couldn't leave," Mr. Wilkerson whispered.

Frank and Joe were stunned. Was that what was in the envelope that Agent Martin told them not to open unless they weren't able to keep the two phony agents from reaching Hidden Mountain?

"Why didn't the FBI agents tell us that?" Joe said. "If we can't stop these two phony FBI agents before we get there, we'll never be able to return to Bayport?"

When Mr. Wilkerson didn't answer, Frank said, "Well, that's all the more reason we *have* to succeed!"

"Hey! We could use some help over here!" Jersey shouted to them.

"I'll help you!" Joe called. He, Frank, and Mr. Wilkerson hurried over to where the two men were trying to get the gear together. "Man, this is exciting!" Joe said. "We were talking about all the things we plan to do when we get to Hidden Mountain."

That seemed to mollify Willy and Jersey.

"If Jersey and Willy reach Hidden Mountain, they'll do away with everyone there," Frank whispered to his brother and Mr. Wilkerson. "We have a plan to stop them, but we'll need your help to implement it."

"You know we'll do what we can, Frank," Mr. Wilkerson whispered.

"Hey—we're ready!" Jersey shouted. "Cut the chatter, and let's get started."

"He must think we're really dumb," Frank whispered. "No FBI agent would talk like that."

"Well, we can't let them know we're too bright," Mr. Wilkerson said as he hefted the pack onto his back. "We just let them talk—that seems to satisfy them."

"Good idea," Frank said.

Finally everyone was ready, and, with Mr. Wilkerson in the lead, they started walking through the forest again.

"We can't take this much time getting ready every morning," Jersey said to no one in particular. "We need to get to Hidden Mountain."

"Frank and I will help with the gear tomorrow morning," Joe said with a pleasant smile. "That'll probably save us all some time."

"That's a good idea," Jersey said. He didn't sound as though he realized that Joe was letting them know that he felt they were slow because of Willy and Joe's ineptitude.

The Hardys and Darren were behind Mr. Wilkerson. Mrs. Wilkerson was just ahead of Willy and Jersey, and was keeping them occupied with stories about how life in the Witness Protection Program differed from city to city. From the short snatches of conversation that Joe could hear, he knew that she was making it all up—but her stories seemed to fascinate Willy and Jersey.

Keep it up, Mrs. Wilkerson, Joe thought. *This will give us that much more time to plan what to do with those guys.*

"I wish you were going to Hidden Mountain with us for real," Darren told them. "I'm not quite sure how this is going to work out."

Frank could hear the sadness in Darren's voice. He could hardly imagine how he'd feel if all of a sudden he were taken from the world of Bayport and sent to live somewhere in the wilderness of British Columbia. He couldn't even imagine what Hidden Mountain was like. He didn't *want* to imagine it.

"There's a reason you have to go there, though," Joe said. "It doesn't sound like there's an alternative solution for keeping you safe."

"There's not, and I know that," Darren said, "and in my mind, I've accepted it—but sometimes, in my heart, well . . . I don't want to sound poetic or anything, but if I think about it too much, I just go crazy."

Suddenly the forest floor got steeper.

"Well, we're out of the easy part," Mr. Wilkerson said. "From here on, according to the agent who visited us, it gets really steep in places."

Frank wondered how Detective Kitimat was making it. What he wanted more than anything was to talk to him, just to assure himself that their father's friend was nearby, because he represented a connection to civilization that Frank felt himself losing. Maybe it was listening to Darren—he didn't know. But he knew that he and Joe needed to do something soon to implement their plan to separate the two phony FBI agents from the Wilkersons.

As if they had read his mind, Willy and Jersey suddenly appeared right behind them.

"We missed your company," Jersey said. He looked at Mrs. Wilkerson. "No offense, but I was getting kind of tired listening to all your chatter."

Joe looked at Frank. He didn't like the way Jersey had suddenly started talking. Surely they knew enough to realize that the Wilkersons would start to get suspicious about them.

But Mrs. Wilkerson said, "Oh, I'm sorry, Agent Sims and Agent Martin. I do that too much. Please forgive me. I'll be quiet and won't say a word."

"Hey! That's okay!" Willy said. "Jersey lives alone and isn't used to so much talking." He paused for a moment. "You know, you can call me Willy. And Agent Martin, he's Jersey."

Mrs. Wilkerson, true to her word, just smiled.

Well done, Frank thought. *She took the blame, so there's no way they'll think they did anything wrong.*

Unfortunately for Frank, though, he was unable to let Joe know what he had been thinking. He'd just have to wait until the two phony FBI agents started falling behind. He hoped it wouldn't be too long. Maybe the elevation would start to take its toll on them.

Higher and higher they climbed. Suddenly a swirling mist began closing in.

"It's hard to see each other in this mess," Willy said. "Should we tie a rope around our waists?"

"These are just clouds," Mr. Wilkerson said. "We'll be in and out of them. Ropes around our waists would be dangerous."

"Yeah, I guess you're right," Willy said.

Way to go, Mr. Wilkerson! Frank thought. *The last thing we need is to be tied to these two—we want to get rid of them.*

Soon they came to a place where rock slides had cut vast swatches of forest all the way to the valley below, and Joe could see in the distance below a blue lake that looked like a jewel in the velvety green forest. He could have stopped there, just to admire the postcard beauty of the scene—but he knew they had more pressing things to do.

Once again they entered a thick mist, which started to play tricks on them as it swirled around their heads.

"Stay together!" Jersey shouted. His voice had a funny ring to it. "Don't get too far ahead."

When nobody answered, Willy said, "Say something! I mean it!"

"Something!" Darren shouted. "What's the matter with you two?"

"Nothing's the matter with us," Jersey shouted. "We're in charge of getting you to Hidden Mountain, so if we lose you, then it's our heads."

Yeah, it'll be your heads all right, Frank thought. *If you don't get rid of everybody, like the crime syndicate has told you to do, then they'll get rid of you.*

Just then a sudden gust of wind almost knocked Joe down. Instinctively he reached out to grab hold of something and knew right away it was one of the two phony FBI agents.

At once, two strong hands grabbed at him and found his throat and began squeezing. He could no longer breath. He started flailing, touching nothing for several seconds, until he finally hit somebody. Whoever it was yelped, then said, "Watch it! What's going on?"

It was Frank!

Joe tried to say something, but he was beginning to black out. He closed his eyes.

From a long way away, he heard a voice say, "Get your hands off him. Just what do you think you're doing?" He thought he recognized Mr. Wilkerson's voice.

Suddenly Joe felt air flowing back into his lungs and he began to gasp for breath.

"What's wrong with you, Jersey?" This time Joe recognized Mrs. Wilkerson's voice. He opened his eyes. The mist had disappeared, and he was looking up into the faces of everyone standing over him.

"Joe?" Frank said. "Are you okay?"

Joe managed to nod. He opened his mouth to say something, but coughed instead. Finally he managed to say, "What happened?"

"It was just Jersey," Willy said, actually looking embarrassed. "He's on edge, and I guess he thought somebody was trying to take him down."

"Good heavens, Jersey," Mrs. Wilkerson said. "Why would one of us want to harm an FBI agent? After all, you're the one who has to make sure we reach Hidden Mountain."

"Yeah, you're right, Mrs. Wilkerson. I'm sorry," Jersey said. "It won't happen again."

"I think we need to rest here for a few minutes," Mr. Wilkerson suggested, "so we can get our bearings again."

Neither Willy nor Jersey disagreed. In fact the two of them retreated several paces away, out of earshot, and sat back down against a tree.

"I think they're beginning to lose it," Mrs. Wilkerson said. "I don't know if we'll make it before one of them cracks."

The Hardy boys looked at each other. They felt the same way.

"How much farther to Hidden Mountain?" Joe asked.

Mr. Wilkerson took a deep breath. "We have another day at least," he told them. "The terrain only gets more rugged from here on out."

"Which means that Willy and Jersey's stress level will only increase," Mrs. Wilkerson said.

Frank looked back down the trail at the two phony FBI agents. They seemed to be engaged in a heated argument. "I hope they're not talking about doing away with us before we get to Hidden Mountain," he said.

13 Falling Rocks

Once again, with incredible speed, the mist swirled in on them—but this time it was much thicker. It was so thick, in fact, that Joe couldn't see the tips of his fingers when he held out his hand.

"We're high enough that we could have a light snow," Mr. Wilkerson said to them.

"I think we'd better stay here until morning," Mrs. Wilkerson suggested. "We don't have that much daylight left, and I certainly don't want to start out in this." She lowered her voice. "I don't care *what* those two say."

"Jersey! Willy!" Mr. Wilkerson shouted at the top of his lungs. "Are you two all right?"

"Yeah, we're fine," Willy called back.

Frank thought his voice seemed closer than it

should be. He didn't know if the wind made it sound that way or if the two phony FBI agents had moved closer to where the Wilkersons and the Hardy boys were.

Suddenly Jersey's face was almost in Joe's. "We thought we had lost you," he said.

Joe turned away because of Jersey's bad breath, but he managed to say, "Where did you think we'd go?"

Neither one of the men said anything.

"We've decided to stay here until morning," Mr. Wilkerson told them. "This weather may not lift for a while, and I don't think it's a good idea to take a chance in this mist."

"That's okay by me," Willy said.

For the next hour, the Wilkersons and the Hardys tried to relax—but having the two phony FBI agents this close to them made it hard.

Finally Mrs. Wilkerson said, "Would anyone like some trail mix?"

"Is that all you've got to eat?" Jersey said irritably. "I'm hungry for a good steak."

"Well, I was thinking about that, Jersey," Joe said. "Frank and I know how to make a bow and arrows, so we could do that and probably bag us a deer. We could then roast it over a big fire."

"Yeah?" Jersey said. "Well, quit talking about it and do it!"

"They're pulling your leg, Jersey," Willy said. "Just eat the trail mix and shut up."

That seemed to quiet everyone down.

The last thing Frank wanted to do was raise the tempers of the two men. "Actually, Joe wasn't kidding, Willy," he said. "We could do that—except the weather's against us. But who knows what might happen tomorrow."

As the evening progressed, the wind seemed to increase, and from time to time it would clear out the mist for short periods of time. Even though the wind wasn't bitterly cold, it was cold enough to chill everyone, so Frank suggested that they all try to find thicker brush to crawl under.

The next time the mist cleared, they all scrambled for whatever thick cover they could see. The Hardys and Darren managed to find a bush together, far enough away from everyone else that they felt free enough to talk openly about what was going on. Frank and Joe soon discovered, however, that everything they mentioned would make Darren think of all the things he would no longer be able to do once he was living permanently at Hidden Mountain. He grew very sad.

Finally the three of them fell quiet, and after a few minutes, Darren drifted off to sleep.

"I feel so sorry for him," Frank said. "It almost makes me want to suggest to Mr. Wilkerson that he let Darren come back to Bayport with us."

"I know, Frank—but that would never work," Joe said. "First of all, his parents would never get to see him again, and that wouldn't be fair. Plus, the crime syndicate bosses would probably figure out a way to kidnap him and force the Wilkersons to escape from Hidden Mountain."

"I hadn't thought about that," Frank said. "You're right."

Joe yawned. "We need to get some sleep too," he said. "We have one more day to take care of our two phony FBI agents, and we need to make sure we're really alert."

"You're right," Frank said. He looked around. "I wonder just how close Detective Kitimat is."

"Pretty close," a voice whispered from the mist.

Frank's head jerked around. "Detective Kitimat?" he whispered.

At that moment Detective Kitimat stuck his head through the underbrush.

"Where'd you come from?" Joe asked.

"I've been trailing you all along," Detective Kitimat said. "I have to say that I'm having a bit of fun re-living my younger days, when I spent weeks at a time in these woods with just a fraction of the supplies I have now!"

"That's good to hear," Frank whispered. "We've been worried about you."

"Oh, you don't need to be worried about me, boys," Detective Kitimat said. "I'm feeling younger every hour. This is just what I needed to get out of the funk I was in."

"Good," Joe said, "but we're not having much luck separating those guys from the Wilkersons."

"I know. I kept thinking we'd be able to get them away eventually," Detective Kitimat said, "but these two guys are either brighter than we give them credit for, or just lucky—I don't know which."

"We don't either," Frank agreed.

"You haven't told the Wilkersons I was trailing you, have you?" Detective Kitimat asked.

Joe looked surprised at the question. "No. We thought that was part of the plan, not to let anyone know you were nearby," Joe said, "just in case it might slip out unexpectedly in a conversation."

"Good. I was just checking to make sure," Detective Kitimat said. "I didn't think you would, but, just as you said, sometimes these things slip out in conversation. I just needed to make sure that we still had that element of surprise."

"We do," Frank told him.

"I need to go back into hiding now," Detective Kitimat said. "I'll be close by, though, in case anything happens."

"That's good to know," Joe told him.

Detective Kitimat crawled backward into the thick underbrush and disappeared.

Frank checked the inside pocket of his coat. "The envelope that Agent Martin gave me is still here," he said.

"Frank, what's inside that envelope scares me," Joe told him. "Agent Martin said that we were only to open it if the two phony FBI agents made it to Hidden Mountain, and then we *had* to obey all of the instructions it gave us."

"I know, Joe. It scares me, too—especially after what Mr. Wilkerson said about our having to stay there forever ourselves," Frank said. "That's why we have to make sure that we separate those two guys from the Wilkersons tomorrow."

A couple of chirping birds woke Frank. The air was crisp and clear, and the sun was shining so brightly that it almost hurt his eyes.

"Up! Up! Up!" Jersey was shouting as he came up the trail toward them. "We've got to get a move on."

Joe couldn't believe how stiff he felt, but he managed to crawl his way out from under the bush and stand up. Mr. and Mrs. Wilkerson were up too, and putting their gear together.

Frank finished packing his gear and started helping Darren, who seemed to be having a hard time waking up. Meanwhile, Mrs. Wilkerson handed out some bags of trail mix, and this time everyone ate it without any complaints. When it was time for them to restart their trip, nobody said anything. Everyone just seemed to fall into their usual routine.

Frank thought he could see anxiety on the faces of Mr. and Mrs. Wilkerson. He was sure that a lot of it had to do with the fact that this was the last day they would spend in the regular world—that by the end of this day, they would be residents of Hidden Mountain and they would never be allowed to leave.

When Darren started lagging behind everyone else, Mrs. Wilkerson dropped back, put her arms around his shoulders, and whispered something in his ear. The two phony FBI agents saw what she was doing, but they didn't comment on it. Joe thought they were too busy thinking about how close they themselves were getting to their final destination.

Higher and higher they climbed, and it was obvious that the air was getting thinner. Finally, after they had gone through a very thick stand of fir trees, they came to an opening with a view that stunned both of the Hardy boys.

Mr. Wilkerson halted. "We're getting close," he said. "It looks like a paradise, doesn't it?"

Frank had to admit that it was one of the most breath-taking views he had ever seen. Meltwater streams trickling from some unseen source gathered on the floor of the forested valley to form the silver strands of a river. A knobby outcrop that hung off the side of a far ridge looked like a gargoyle on a French cathedral. "It reminds me of a book we read in English class," he said. *Lost Horizon*."

Mrs. Wilkerson smiled at him. "When I knew we were coming here, I bought a copy of that and read it twice," she said. "It really helped me come to terms with what we're doing."

"How much farther is it?" Willy said.

"We have to go down into that valley, follow the river for a couple of miles, and then we'll see it," Mr. Wilkerson said. Without waiting for one of the phoney FBI agents to say it, he added, "So let's get started. I'll lead the way, and Willy will bring up the rear."

The next hundred yards were down a gentle slope, but then the descent became treacherous. It was all open, too, and the Hardy boys realized that there was no way Detective Kitimat could stay close to them now. He'd just have to wait until they reached the valley, then try to make it down without being observed. It would be tricky at best, Joe knew, but if anyone could do it, it was Detective Kitimat.

As they slowly made their way down to the valley, Joe maneuvered himself next to Frank. "Maybe we could give them a little push—just enough to break something when they fall, so that they couldn't continue," he suggested. "What do you think?"

"Our job is to detain them for the authorities, not hurt them," Frank whispered back. "That's the predicament we're in here, Joe."

"Just a thought, Frank," Joe said testily. "We're running out of time!"

"I know we are, and I'm thinking as fast as I can about what we can do," Frank replied. "I don't

130

want to know the contents of that envelope any more than you do."

"That's exactly what I *do* want to know," Joe said.

"Why?" Frank asked. "We're not supposed to open it unless the two phony FBI agents reach Hidden Mountain."

"Well, Frank, I think it's very likely that's going to happen," Joe said, "so if we know the contents of that letter now, maybe we'll be able to make some additional plans."

Frank looked around to see if Willy would be able to tell what he was doing, but he realized that Willy was too busy making sure he didn't fall down the mountain.

Frank withdrew the envelope, hurriedly opened it, gasped, then quickly thrust it to Joe for a quick read.

"I suspected something like this," Joe said. "Now we know how to deal with the situation."

"You got any really good suggestions?" Frank asked.

"Well, we need to make sure that both Willy and Jersey are behind us when we get there," Joe said. "I think we need to do that now."

"I'll follow your lead, then," Frank said.

"Hey, Jersey—my brother and I have changed our minds," Joe shouted. "We want to turn back!"

"What?" Jersey said. "What do you mean?"

"Well, we've decided that we don't want to do

131

this after all," Joe continued, "so we're just going to go back to Bayport. You guys can go on."

Suddenly Willy pulled a gun from his waist and pointed it at the Hardy boys. "I don't think so," he said. "Now start walking."

"Hey!" Joe shouted. "You can't do this to us."

"Just watch me," Willy said. "Jersey! Get back up here! Our plans have changed." Willy waved his gun in the air.

Jersey took out his gun and pointed it at the Wilkersons, who seemed genuinely surprised to see it—even though they knew who Willy and Jersey really were.

Jersey herded the Wilkersons back up the slope to where Willy was standing with the Hardy boys.

"What's going on here?" Mr. Wilkerson demanded.

"Shut up!" Jersey said.

"Nothing's going on here," Willy said. "We're taking all of you to Hidden Mountain, but now we'll be behind you—so if you try anything, your final resting place will be where you choose it to be."

Without a word, the Wilkersons joined hands, turned around, and started back down the mountain.

"What are you two waiting for?" Jersey shouted to the Hardy boys. "Get going!"

Frank and Joe did as they were ordered.

Joe knew that the two phony FBI agents would have trouble maneuvering down the slope and that he and Frank could get close enough to the

Wilkersons to let them know that this was all part of their plan.

"This will work," Joe whispered. "We just need to stay as close together as possible."

"We need to keep as much distance as we can between us and Willy and Jersey," Frank added, "but not enough to make them suspicious."

"Hey, slow down!" Jersey shouted. "I'll send a bullet your way if you don't."

"When they tell us to slow down, we need to slow down," Joe whispered, "but then, after a few minutes, we need to put a little more distance between us and them until they tell us to slow down again."

Finally the Hardy boys and the Wilkersons reached the bottom of the valley. Willy and Jersey were still making their way down the slopes.

"Slow down!" Jersey shouted again.

"I have an idea. I'll fall back, but you guys keep going," Joe whispered. "If they see one of us dropping back, they might not get so agitated."

Joe slowed his pace, which seemed to placate Willy and Jersey—but as soon as they reached the valley floor, he started walking a little faster and was soon close enough to Frank that he could talk to him without being heard by the two phony FBI agents.

"Once we start up Hidden Mountain, I don't think Willy and Jersey will worry about how fast we're climbing," Joe whispered. "For all they know, everyone still thinks they're the real thing, so they won't be expecting what's in store for them."

"Let's hope you're right," Frank whispered back.

Just then the river bank turned sharply. Within a few feet, they had reached a sight that very few people on Earth had ever seen.

Towering above them was a side of a mountain that looked as though it had been sheered away by a huge knife. About halfway up was a city—or at least the facade of a city. Houses, many of them looking just like ones in Bayport, had been built into its side. From where they were standing, it looked as though streets leading from house to house had been carved out too.

But, Frank and Joe realized, between where they were standing and their final destination lay some of the most treacherous mountain climbing they had ever seen.

"Well, this is it," Mr. Wilkerson said. "This is what we trained for."

The Wilkersons started up the side of the mountain. Behind them were the Hardys.

Willy and Jersey were still several yards below, but now Frank was surprised to see that instead of being rank amateurs, the two phony FBI agents seemed to know exactly what they were doing as they began preparing for the climb.

"We may be in a lot of trouble here if we don't get higher up the mountain before they start up,"

Frank said to the Wilkersons. "Try to climb faster."

For a while they seemed to be getting ahead of Willy and Jersey—but then it suddenly appeared that the two phony FBI agents found their rhythm, and they began catching up.

"This isn't good," Frank whispered to Joe. "This isn't good at all."

Just then Joe looked above them and saw movement among several huge boulders just below the houses on the side of the cliff. He quickly glanced down at Willy and Jersey. The two men were now in an unprotected place on the side of the mountain. Just above the Hardys and the Wilkersons were a couple of huge rock overhangs.

"Head for those!" Joe shouted. "We don't have any time to lose."

At that moment, the huge boulders that Joe had been looking at a few seconds ago began cascading down the mountain toward them.

14 Hidden Mountain

The Hardy boys and the Wilkersons reached the rock overhangs just before the boulders rained down.

Joe could hear Willy and Jersey shouting frantically, but he didn't have time to look around to see exactly what was happening to them. Fortunately their shelter went far enough back into the side of the mountain that they were protected when the overhangs broke off and fell down the side of the mountain.

When Frank finally looked back down, all he could see was a pile of huge boulders at the base of the mountain. Willy and Jersey were gone.

"Those poor men," Mrs. Wilkerson said.

Mr. Wilkerson looked at her. "What do you

mean?" he said. "They were prepared to hurt us."

"I know that's true," Mrs. Wilkerson said, "but I still can't keep from wondering where their lives took a wrong turn."

Mr. Wilkerson patted his wife's arm and then looked at the Hardys. "I'm curious," he said. "How did you manage to make sure that what happened to Willy and Jersey didn't happen to us?"

Frank took the top-secret letter out of his pocket and handed it to Mr. Wilkerson. "One of the real FBI agents gave this to us before they had to leave," he explained. "We were only to open it if Willy and Jersey made it to Hidden Mountain."

Mr. Wilkerson quickly read the letter. "Oh, my goodness! It suggests a way to separate yourself from people who aren't supposed to be coming—but it doesn't guarantee that you won't be killed with them."

Joe nodded. "We weren't supposed to read it until we got to Hidden Mountain, but we decided to read it right before so we could be prepared," he said. "I'm glad we did—because as it turned out, we had to act fast."

"We knew when we started climbing up the mountain that those boulders would rain down on us," Frank added, "but Joe and I had already decided that the five of us weren't going to meet the same fate as Willy and Jersey."

"I'm glad Frank and Joe were along, Mom,"

Darren said. "We wouldn't be here if they weren't."

"Those are the rules of life at Hidden Mountain, I guess. A few might have to be sacrificed to save the lives of many," Mr. Wilkerson said. He sighed. "Well, we still have a long climb ahead of us. We need to get started."

"Wait, Dad," Darren said. "What about Frank and Joe? Why are they going with us?"

Mr. Wilkerson looked at the Hardys.

"Your father didn't tell you the rest of the letter," Joe said. "We have to have permission from the Supreme Council to leave once we've seen Hidden Moutain."

"We're not special FBI agents, Darren. We don't have the clearance needed," Frank said. "Joe and I accepted that when Agents Martin and Sims couldn't complete their mission."

"But you saved our lives," Darren protested. "You've proven that you can be trusted."

"It doesn't matter," Joe said. "Those are the rules, and we accepted them."

Mr. Wilkerson had already climbed out from under what was left of the massive overhang and he looked toward the houses on the side of Hidden Mountain.

"Do you see anybody?" Mrs. Wilkerson called to him.

"No, but we won't see anybody until we get there, I'm sure," Mr. Wilkerson replied. "I know they see us, though, and they're probably wondering who among us survived—so we need to let them know we're all right."

Soon the Hardys, Darren, and Mrs. Wilkerson were out in the open—visible enough that Joe was sure whomever was watching them could tell that they had survived the massive rock slide. With Mr. Wilkerson in the lead, they started back up the mountain.

Joe was surprised that the rest of the climb wasn't as treacherous as he had expected, but it was still challenging—as they had to climb up and down massive boulders, some piled one on top of the other. He could only surmise how Hidden Mountain had been formed, perhaps during some ancient cataclysmic activity in the area. The core of the Earth must have spit up thousands and thousands of these boulders so that they collected one on top of the other—like pockmarks on the face of the mountain.

"I certainly hope that none of the other boulders is loose," Mrs. Wilkerson said. "I don't see any place to hide from another rock slide."

"I think they must have this pretty well figured out," Frank told her. "I've noticed some spots that look as though traps have been laid."

"What do you mean?" Mr. Wilkerson said.

"Some of these piles of boulders are ready to rain down on anyone who starts up this mountain uninvited," Joe said. "It's very ingenious how they've done it."

"Could we accidentally set them loose?" Darren asked. "What if we trip over something?"

"Don't worry about it, Darren," Frank said. "It's a very sophisticated setup."

"That's good to know," Mrs. Wilkerson said.

For the next hour, everyone concentrated on conserving their oxygen. The air was beginning to get thinner. Once Darren started coughing, and everyone stopped to let him get his breath. Mrs. Wilkerson had a concerned look on her face.

"Your body adjusts to the altitude," Frank said. "It may take a few days, but after a while you won't notice it."

"It's not far now," Mr. Wilkerson said. "I'm surprised that we've not seen anyone yet."

Actually, Joe was surprised too. He thought by now there would be a welcoming party—but maybe something like that only happened in the movies or on television.

Just then, a man with graying hair, dressed in what looked like work clothes, appeared at the door of the nearest house. He watched the group climb for a few more minutes, then he waved.

Everyone waved back.

"Well, that's a good sign, I guess," Mrs. Wilkerson said.

In a few minutes, a woman and a small child

came to stand beside the man. He didn't take his eyes off the group as they climbed up the last few yards that still separated them from what looked like the start of a street carved into the side of the mountain. Finally, when they were within a few feet of the house door, the man said, "Welcome to Hidden Mountain. I'm Angus Hardesty. I'm more or less the official gatekeeper."

"We're glad to be here, finally," Mr. Wilkerson said.

"You're home," the woman behind Angus Hardesty said. "I'm Anne. This is our daughter, Melinda, and this is"—she stood aside to let a boy who looked the same age as Darren and the Hardys stand next to Mr. Hardesty—"our son, Jonathan."

Jonathan nodded politely, but Joe could tell that he kept his eyes on Darren. *He's glad that somebody new his own age is here,* he thought, *so he can find out what's going on in the world he left behind.*

"You'll all need to follow us," Angus said. "I know you're tired, but there are formalities to be taken care of."

"We understand," Mr. Wilkerson said.

As they stepped into the doorway of the Hardestys' house, Frank was stunned by what he saw. It could have been a house anywhere in suburbia. In a way, it reminded him of their house in Bayport. But the thing that surprised Frank the most was that the house had "windows." Behind the sheer curtains, he could see the outlines of trees and even of houses across the street, but he knew he was just seeing an illusion. He wondered how in the world whoever had built this house had been able to do it.

With the Hardestys leading the way, they went through a back door and stepped into a world that now reminded Joe of the narrow streets he and his family had seen in medieval European cities. Bordering the street were the facades of houses out of the latest issue of an architecture magazine. It was amazing, Joe thought. He started to say something to Darren, but he saw that he and Jonathan were talking animatedly about something—and he didn't want to interrupt them. Joe was just glad to see Darren coming out of his despondency.

They continued up the narrow street. People appeared in the doorways of their houses or looked out the windows and waved, but no one said anything.

Finally they reached the end of the street, turned a corner, and started up an incline. The road they were now on ended abruptly at the door of a facade that looked like an official building.

"This is the Registry Building," Mr. Hardesty said. "We'll leave you here—but I'm sure that we'll be talking to you soon."

"Thank you very much for welcoming us," Mr. Wilkerson said.

"I'll talk to you later, Darren," Jonathan said. "I'll

have you over, and I'll start introducing you to everyone."

"That's great," Darren said.

Mr. Wilkerson opened the door, and everyone stepped inside. The interior of the Registry Building looked like something out of a space movie. There were computers and television monitors everywhere. One wall was covered with a huge map of the world.

A woman sitting behind a desk just inside the entry looked up and gave them a smile. "Robert! Sandra! Darren! Welcome to Hidden Mountain. I'm Julia Sonntag. We've been expecting you." She looked at Frank and Joe and added, "But I'm afraid the Supreme Council will need to meet about your two young friends here." She looked at her watch. "A session is slated to start in about five minutes." She stood up. "In the meantime, you'll all need to be debriefed—but I want to make you as comfortable as possible. Won't you follow me?"

Mrs. Sonntag led everyone down a long hallway to another door, opened it, stepped away so everyone could enter, and then followed and shut the door. "This will be your home for a few weeks, until you decide where you want to live."

Frank and Joe looked around. They were in an apartment that could have been in a high-rise in some major American city. Across the luxuriously appointed living room, Frank could see the nighttime skyline of some major city. He couldn't recognize any landmarks, such as the Empire State Building, so he thought it might just be a generic skyline—but he was impressed just the same. He was amazed at how the mind could play tricks on people and make them believe they were somewhere else instead of inside an isolated mountain in the wilderness of northern British Columbia.

"Incredible," Darren said.

"Yes, it is, isn't it?" Mrs. Sonntag said. "Just make yourselves comfortable." She gave them another big smile and left the apartment.

Darren walked over and turned on the television set. One of the season's top sitcoms appeared.

"Oh, man! I've been wondering if I'd ever get to see this again," Darren said. He looked over at Frank and Joe. "Come on. Let's watch it!"

Since Frank and Joe enjoyed the comedy too, they joined Darren on the huge couch in front of the television set.

In the middle of the program the doorbell rang, and Mr. Wilkerson went to answer it.

Three men with briefcases asked if they could come in to visit with him. With only a moment's hesitation, to adjust to the fact that this was now their apartment, Mr. Wilkerson said, "Of course."

Even with all the incredible surprises they had seen so far, the Hardys were anxious about their situation, so both Frank and Joe tried to listen to as

144

much of Mr. and Mrs. Wilkerson's conversation with the three men as possible. The television was loud, but Joe was able to pick up his and Frank's names from time to time, so he knew that in addition to the debriefing, the fate of the Hardy boys was also being discussed.

Finally Darren said, "I'm hungry. What about you guys?"

It was then that Frank realized just how famished he really was. He turned to Joe. "I am. What about you?"

"Well, do we order out, or do you think the kitchen is fully stocked?" Joe asked.

"This is our apartment," Darren said. "I suppose it's all right for us to start opening cabinets and refrigerator doors."

Just as the three of them stood up, Mr. Wilkerson said, "Frank, Joe—we need to talk to you."

The Hardys looked at each other. Together they realized that the moment of truth had come.

Frank and Joe walked over to where the three men were sitting with Mr. and Mrs. Wilkerson.

All three men stood up and smiled at the boys, and they all shook hands.

"We know your father very well," one of the men said. "In fact he helped me get into my first Witness Protection Program."

Frank nodded. He knew this was not a place to ask questions. In fact it hadn't been lost on them that none of the three men had told them their names.

"The Supreme Council has met and decided that the sons of Fenton Hardy can be trusted to keep the secret of Hidden Mountain," one of the other men said. "You'll stay here with the Wilkersons tonight, but you will leave early in the morning so that you can make it down Hidden Mountain, retrace your journey back along the river and over the next mountain, and then radio the FBI helicopter to pick you up."

"No air traffic of any kind is allowed within fifty miles of Hidden Mountain," Mr. Wilkerson said. "I wish we could send a helicopter to have you picked up from here."

"That's no problem," Frank said. "Joe and I can make it just fine."

Joe nodded. "We'll be all right," he added.

"You are your father's sons," all three men said.

"I think Darren's waiting for you to raid the kitchen," Mrs. Wilkerson said.

The Hardys grinned. This was the last night they'd ever spend with their friend, so they were going to make the most of it.

15 Witness Protection

It was almost 5 A.M. when the Hardy boys finally got back to Bayport. In three hours they'd be back in their classrooms at Bayport High School.

Just as Joe started to unlock the front door, it opened. Mr. Hardy was there to welcome them home.

"It's great to see you, Dad!" the Hardy boys whispered.

"It's great to see you, too, sons," Mr. Hardy said. "I had a telephone call from Rupert Kitimat late last night. Although he didn't give me all the details, I understand you're lucky to be here at all."

"We've always known that the Hardy name was respected by a lot of people around the world, Dad," Frank said, "but I don't think that either Joe or I realized just how deep that respect went."

Joe nodded.

"Do you want to sleep some more," Mr. Hardy asked, "or do you want to have a little breakfast and tell me about what happened?"

Frank looked at Joe. "I think it would probably take me a while to go back to sleep," he said, "and then I'd feel miserable when I woke up—so I say we eat and talk."

"Sounds good to me," Joe agreed.

Frank and Joe followed their father into the kitchen and were immediately surprised by the spread they saw on the table.

"Is Mom up?" Frank asked.

"Not yet," Mr. Hardy said. "I did this myself!"

"You did *this*?" Joe said, looking at the pancakes, bacon, scrambled eggs, and slices of cantaloupe.

"How in the world do you think I survived before I married your mother?" Mr. Hardy said. He looked admiringly at the food on the table. "Frankly I was quite pleased to find out that I hadn't lost my touch."

"Well, it certainly *looks* good," Frank said, "but the ultimate test is how it *tastes*."

"I've already tasted it," Mr. Hardy said, smirking. "It's pretty good, if I do say so myself."

"Well, then, with a recommendation like that," Joe said, "what are we waiting for?"

The three of them sat down at the table, and the boys began filling their plates.

After Frank and Joe had taken several bites of their food, they pronounced their father a gourmet cook.

"Parents are full of surprises," Joe said.

"Well, so are children," Mr. Hardy told them. "Why don't you tell me about everything that happened?"

For the next hour, Frank and Joe took turns telling their father everything that happened to them, from the time they left Bayport until the current moment.

After they were told by the Supreme Council of Hidden Mountain that they could return home, they had spent a fascinating evening with Darren and Jonathan and some friends. When they had been outside the houses in Hidden Mountain, they had felt transported back in time, when certain civilizations lived in similar circumstances on the sides of mountains. But when they had gone inside the various buildings, they were once again in the twenty-first century. Jonathan had taken them to a large sports complex with ice skating and tennis and basketball courts. They had watched professional soccer and baseball games beamed to them by satellite. When school was in session, Jonathan had told them, he played several sports himself. Without being asked, Jonathan had admitted that sometimes he thought about what life was like off of Hidden Mountain—but when he thought about leaving, he hadn't wanted to.

The next morning Frank and Joe had said a sad

farewell to the Wilkersons and were taken to the Hardesty's house. They left through the door they had first used to enter Hidden Mountain, and were soon making their way back into the woods.

When they reached the huge pile of boulders that they knew had entombed Willy and Jersey, they hadn't stopped. Instead they had quickly found the river, followed it until they were out of sight of Hidden Mountain, and then started up the side of the next mountain. Within a couple of hours, they had reached the peak, then started their next descent—and that's when they had run into Detective Kitimat.

"It was like finding a long-lost friend," Joe said. "He was really glad to see us."

"I can imagine," Mr. Hardy said.

"We didn't know where we'd find him," Frank said, "or even *if* we'd find him."

"He said he felt totally helpless when he watched us go down the side of that mountain with the Wilkersons and the two phony FBI agents," Joe said, "but there was no protection, so he couldn't follow us."

Since they still weren't fifty miles away from Hidden Mountain, they'd had to walk farther down the mountain. Then Detective Kitimat had used his cell phone to radio the FBI helicopter, which had picked the three of them up and had taken them to Dawson Creek.

From there Frank and Joe caught a flight to Vancouver, British Columbia, connected with an Air Canada flight to Toronto, and then boarded another Air Canada flight to JFK.

"You hold a great secret, sons," Mr. Hardy told them. "Will it be too heavy a burden for you?"

"We're Hardys, Dad," Frank said seriously. "We can handle it."

Joe nodded. "We certainly can," he said.

Just as they started to get up from the table, Mrs. Hardy came into the kitchen.

"Oh, it is so good to see you boys," Mrs. Hardy said. "I've missed you. But I guess you had a really exciting time, hiking in the woods and everything!"

"'Exciting' would be one way to describe it, Mom," Frank said with a grin. Clearly, his dad had kept the mission secret from their mom—probably so that she wouldn't be too worried. Frank and Joe gave her a big hug, then they went to their room and started getting ready for school.

As they pulled out of their driveway, Joe noticed a black car start up and began following them. He mentioned it to Frank.

"Government?" Frank said.

"Could be," Joe said. "Maybe they just want to make sure we're all right."

After a few minutes, Frank said, "Maybe."

But Joe didn't think he sounded too convinced.

When they got to the school parking lot, Frank

pulled into a space next to Chet's car, and he and Joe got out of the van.

"Don't look at the car," Frank whispered. "Just act normal."

As they started up the sidewalk toward the front door, Joe said, "There's something about this that doesn't feel right, Frank. I think we need to let Dad know about it."

"I agree," Frank said.

When they got inside the school, Joe took out his cell phone, turned it on, and dialed their father's office phone. Mr. Hardy answered it after several rings.

"Someone followed us to school, Dad," Joe said. "There's a black car parked on the street at the edge of the student lot. Could you have it checked out? Something about it doesn't feel right to me and Frank."

"I'll do it as soon as I hang up," Mr. Hardy said. "You did the right thing to call."

The boys parted in the main hall. Joe headed to English, and Frank headed to social studies.

When the lunch bell rang, Joe went to the cafeteria to meet Frank. Just as he got there, the principal walked up to them and said, "Your father's in my office, boys. He needs to see you."

Frank and Joe followed the principal to his office. When they stepped inside, they saw their father and two other men.

"I'll leave you alone," the principal said.

"Thank you," Mr. Hardy said.

Frank and Joe sat down in a couple of side chairs.

"This is Agent Collins and Agent Morrow," Mr. Hardy said.

Frank and Joe nodded.

"The two men in the black car have been taken into custody," Mr. Hardy continued. "They were members of the same crime syndicate that was trying to find the Wilkersons. The FBI is sure that they were planning to kidnap you two, to try to force you to tell them how to get to Hidden Mountain."

Joe felt a chill go through him. "What does this mean?" he asked.

"Unfortunately, it means that the two of you will have around the clock FBI surveillance until we're satisfied that no more members of this particular crime family will try to kidnap you," Agent Morrow said.

"Well, what about other crime families?" Frank said. "Will it end with this particular one, or will they give the information to other people?"

"That's not the way it usually works," Agent Collins said. "There's no history of that happening."

Agent Morrow nodded his agreement. "They don't usually share this kind of information," he said. "We see no reason to believe it'll happen this time."

"You boys will have to be very vigilant for a while," Mr. Hardy said. "It'll certainly mean an adjustment to your lifestyle, but I have faith that the FBI will make sure nothing happens to you."

The boys shook hands with the men, said good-bye to their father, and left the principal's office.

"How are we going to handle this?" Joe asked as they headed toward their next class.

"Well, first I need to stop at the snack machine to get something to eat, since we didn't get to have lunch," Frank said. "I can't fight crime on an empty stomach."

Joe laughed. "I guess it's good that we can have a sense of humor about this," he said.

"Well, I'll tell you," Frank said, taking some money out of his pocket for the machine, "we'll just watch our backs. Because the only alternative is going to live at Hidden Mountain. It might be a fun place to visit—but I wouldn't want to spend the rest of my life there."

"I agree," Joe said. He took some coins out of his pocket and put them into the machine. "We've been fighting crime long enough to know how to survive," he added. "We can outlast this family of crooks."

Frank took a bite of his candy bar. "You said it!" he said.

"I'll meet you in the parking lot after school."

Joe nodded. "Just be careful," he said.

"Sure will," Frank said.